HEAT AND DUST

'The past is a foreign country,' said a famous writer, 'they

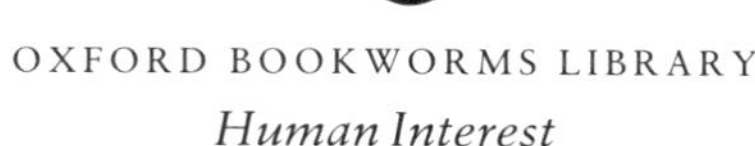

OXFORD BOOKWORMS LIBRARY

Human Interest

Heat and Dust

Stage 5 (1800 headwords)

Series Editor: Jennifer Bassett
Founder Editor: Tricia Hedge
Activities Editors: Jennifer Bassett and Alison Baxter

RUTH PRAWER JHABVALA

Heat and Dust

Retold by
Clare West

OXFORD UNIVERSITY PRESS

Oxford University Press
Great Clarendon Street, Oxford OX2 6DP

Oxford New York
Athens Auckland Bangkok Bogotá Buenos Aires Cape Town
Chennai Dar es Salaam Delhi Florence Hong Kong Istanbul Karachi
Kolkata Kuala Lumpur Madrid Melbourne Mexico City Mumbai Nairobi
Paris São Paulo Shanghai Singapore Taipei Tokyo Toronto Warsaw
with associated companies in
Berlin Ibadan

OXFORD and OXFORD ENGLISH
are trade marks of Oxford University Press

ISBN 0 19 423068 6

Third impression 2001

First published in Oxford Bookworms 1990
This second edition published in the Oxford Bookworms Library 2000

The publishers would like to thank the following for their permission to reproduce illustrations:
Heat and Dust, Merchant Ivory Productions; The Kobal Collection

Printed in Spain by Unigraf s.l.

CONTENTS

PEOPLE IN THIS STORY

DIARY OF THE 1970s

Diary-writer (unnamed), *granddaughter of Douglas Rivers*
Inder Lal, *her landlord in Satipur*
Ritu, *Inder Lal's wife*
Inder Lal's mother
Maji, *friend of Inder Lal's mother*
Dr Gopal, *Indian doctor at the hospital in Satipur*
Karim, *the Nawab's nephew, living in London*
Kitty, *also Indian, Karim's wife*
Chid (Chidananda), *an Englishman interested in Indian religion*

1923 – OLIVIA'S STORY

Olivia, *first wife of Douglas Rivers*
Douglas Rivers, *assistant British official in Satipur and husband (1) of Olivia, and (2) of Tessie (Beth Crawford's sister)*
Mr Crawford, *chief British official in Satipur*
Beth Crawford, *his wife*
Tessie, *Beth's sister, and second wife of Douglas*
Dr Saunders, *the British doctor*
Joan Saunders, *his wife*
Major Arthur Minnies, *political agent appointed to advise the Nawab*
Mary Minnies, *his wife*
Harry, *the Nawab's friend and guest*
Marcia, *Olivia's sister, living in France and later in England*
The Nawab, *the Indian prince of Khatm, a state 15 miles away from Satipur*
The Begum, *his mother*
Sandy (Zahira) Cabobpur, *his wife, living away from him*

Introduction

This is not my story, it's Olivia's. I've always wanted to know more about her, and especially about that year in her life when her whole world changed. That was 1923.

I only know what happened afterwards, so I'll start there. Olivia was the first wife of my grandfather, Douglas Rivers, and they lived in Satipur, in India, when the British were in control. Douglas was assistant to Mr Crawford, who was the chief British official in the district. They lived in a close circle of British friends, who were all extremely shocked when Olivia left her husband in September 1923 and ran away to live with the Nawab, an Indian prince. Douglas, however, did not show his feelings at all, but remained calm and controlled. He worked harder than ever, keeping law and order. Everyone said he had excellent self-control.

Later that year, Douglas met Tessie, Beth Crawford's sister, who came to stay with the Crawfords in Satipur. Douglas and Tessie spent some time together riding and playing tennis. Tessie stayed over a year in Satipur and then returned to England. Douglas visited her in England a year later. When he got his divorce from Olivia, he and Tessie got married. She joined him in India, and like her sister Beth, she had a full and happy life there. She and Douglas had a son, my father, but of course by the time I was born, India had become independent, and they had all come back to England.

What happened in early 1923 is a mystery. Did Olivia really love Douglas? How did she become interested in the Nawab? What made her finally leave Douglas and live with the Nawab for the rest of her life? And in the end, did she find happiness?

I don't remember my grandfather Douglas at all (he died when I was three), but I do remember Tessie and Beth. They were cheerful,

This is Olivia's story – the story of 1923, the year when her whole life changed.

sensible old ladies, but they refused to talk about Olivia for years. They did not even want to hear her name in conversation. They seemed to think she was almost a criminal. I was always eager to find out more about her, but it was only after their husbands had died that they began to feel free to talk about her.

By that time they had also met Harry again, who knew the Nawab and Olivia well. Harry never visited the sisters while Douglas was alive but he came after Douglas's death, and they talked about Olivia. Harry told them that Olivia's sister, Marcia, had died and left him all Olivia's letters, which he gave to Tessie and Beth. They gave me the letters because I was so interested in Olivia's story.

So I came to India in February this year, bringing the letters with me. I wanted to discover more about life in the 1970s in this strange country, and about the events of 1923. Although I arrived fifty years after Olivia, she and I are alike in many ways, and have shared similar experiences.

It was a good thing that I kept a diary during my first months here. If I tried to remember now what happened then, my memory of it might be different, because *I* am different now. India always changes people, and India has certainly changed me. But this is *Olivia's* story, not mine.

Diary 2 February

My first few days in India

I have arrived in Bombay. It looks so modern, so different from what I had imagined. I've been reading about the India of Olivia's time, in the 1920s, and I was expecting it to be like that. But it isn't! And she arrived by ship, but of course I came by plane. Now there are more people, more buildings, more cars – I must forget what I've read and get used to the India of the 1970s.

I stayed in the missionaries' guesthouse for a few days. On my first night in India, I suddenly woke up about midnight, looked for my watch and couldn't find it. 'Oh no!' I thought. 'Everyone says India is full of thieves. Has someone stolen something from me already?'

A voice called from the next bed: 'Here it is, my dear. You must learn to be more careful in India.'

I sat up in bed and took the watch gratefully.

My neighbour in the next bed said, 'I expect you've just arrived, and that's why you're so careless. You'll learn. There are two things to remember in India. First, keep your watch and your money hidden. Second, never eat food sold in the street, and drink boiled water only. But the food here in the guesthouse is good English food – it's quite safe to eat. I hate Indian food myself.'

I looked at her. The light from the street lamps outside shone in through the uncurtained window, and made her look thin and paper-white, like a ghost.

'I've been a missionary in India for thirty years,' she said, 'and if God wants me to die here, I will.' As she said that, her voice was strong, not like a ghost's at all. 'I've seen terrible sights in India, fighting, disease, and hunger, and I've learnt one thing. You can't live in India without Christ Jesus. He must be with you every moment of the day. Because you see, dear, nothing human means anything here. Not a thing.' As she spoke, her voice was firm and her back was straight. She looked like a ghost, but she was strong. She was like a Hindu – her religion was more important to her than anything else.

Diary 16 February

My new home in Satipur

I'm in Satipur. I've already found a room, which is large and airy. It's over a shop. I pay rent to an Indian government official called Inder Lal, who lives with his wife, mother and children in some small rooms behind the shop. My room is very empty because I have no furniture except a small desk, where I put my diary, Olivia's letters and my Hindi textbook. There is no chair or bed; I sit on the floor and sleep in a sleeping bag. I like the room like this, but Inder Lal keeps looking round for furniture. He can't understand why I want to live such a simple Indian life. But he is so polite that he just says, 'I'm afraid this is not very comfortable for you,' and won't look straight at me. This is not the behaviour he expects from an Englishwoman.

Olivia was very different from me. As soon as she and Douglas moved into their house in Satipur, she filled it with pictures, carpets and flowers. I've already seen the house where Douglas and Olivia lived. After Indian independence in 1947, the British officials' houses were turned into offices, so Olivia's beautiful home now contains several government departments, and Indian officials work in her elegant sitting room.

Diary 20 February

I meet Inder Lal's family

This morning I visited Inder Lal's wife, Ritu, and his mother in their home. I wonder if they always live like this. It was very untidy. The rooms are very small, of course, and there are three young children. I wanted to sit on the floor like them, but they offered me a chair, and clearly thought I should sit like a European. The older woman told Ritu to bring something to eat and drink, and Ritu left the room. So Inder Lal's mother and I smiled at each other, and made signs with our hands. I tried to speak Hindi (without much success – I must work harder at it!). We couldn't understand each other at all. But all the time she was studying me. I can imagine how she had looked carefully at girls as possible wives for her son, before choosing Ritu.

Everyone looks at me curiously in India. They are quite open about it, women as well as men. Sometimes people laugh at me, and they never bother to hide their laughter. I suppose I seem strange to them. I expect they also think it's strange that I, a European, live *with* them, eat their food, and even wear Indian clothes (I wear them because they're cooler and cheaper).

Diary 24 February

Inder Lal and I visit the Palace

As today was Sunday, my landlord, Inder Lal, kindly offered to take me to Khatm to show me the palace of the Nawab, Olivia's Indian prince. I was very eager to see his old home, and discover more about him.

We went by bus. Buses are always the same in India, very old and full of people and with a lot of luggage on top. The scenery doesn't change either. Between one town and another there is nothing but flat land, burning sky, heat and dust. There is a lot of dust. The buses have no windows – they are open at the sides so that hot winds blow in freely, filling your nose and ears and mouth with sand from the desert.

The town of Khatm is very small, with narrow, dirty streets. It's a sad little place, hiding in the shadow of the Nawab's great house. You can see his Palace behind high pearl-grey walls, in large gardens with tall trees, pools and fountains. Inder Lal and I had to wait while someone found the keys. The Palace is locked because it's empty; the royal family all left years ago. I asked Inder Lal about the Nawab's family, but he doesn't know much more than I do. The Nawab died in 1953, and because he had no children, Karim, his nephew, who was a baby then, inherited the Palace. But he never lived there. In fact he lives in London, where I met him just before coming to India (I will write about that later).

Inder Lal didn't want to discuss the Nawab's life. 'I've heard about him,' he said. 'He led a bad life. And I remember something about the scandal with the Englishwoman. But who cares about that now? Nobody is interested in those people any more – they are all dead.' He was much more interested in telling me about his own life. 'Now *I* have many difficulties, so many problems in my office, for example. . .' He went on talking as we entered the Palace.

It was white and cool inside. I saw all the huge halls and rooms I have read about in Olivia's letters, but I couldn't imagine people living there. There were one or two broken sofas, and a silk curtain heavy with dust and age. I touched it but it felt like something dead. It made me feel sad. There was nothing left of that rich, important family. We left the Palace, walking through the cool green garden, and caught the bus home.

1923
Olivia meets the Nawab

The first time Olivia met the Nawab was at a dinner party he gave at the Palace. By that time she had been in Satipur for several months, and was already beginning to get bored. Her husband, Douglas, was extremely busy with his work all day, so Olivia was alone in her big house with all the doors and windows shut to keep out the heat and dust. She read, and played the piano, but the days were long, very long. In the evenings and on Sundays she and Douglas spent time together or visited other British officials and their wives. So the only people she saw were Mr and Mrs Crawford, Dr and Mrs Saunders (Dr Saunders was the British doctor), and Major and Mrs Minnies (Major Minnies was the political agent appointed by the British to advise the Nawab).

On the day of the Nawab's dinner party, Douglas and Olivia were driven to Khatm by the Crawfords in their car. It was about fifteen miles away. Douglas and the Crawfords had visited the Nawab before and had not particularly enjoyed the entertainment. They felt it was their duty to accept the Nawab's invitation but were not looking forward to the evening. Olivia, however, was excited. She had an elegant evening dress to wear, and she wanted to meet new people, who would notice how pretty she was.

Like many Indian princes, the Nawab enjoyed inviting Europeans to dinner. His palace, built in the 1820s, was rather grand. When Olivia saw the enormous dining room, full of beautiful flowers, glass and silver, she was delighted, and felt that at last she had come to the right place in India.

Only the guests were not right. The same people as usual were there, as well as an Englishman called Harry something, who was staying with the Nawab. The Crawfords and the Minnies had been in India for over twenty years, and knew everything about it. Their parents and grandparents had lived in India too. Whenever they met, they discussed people and events from the past. But Olivia was extremely bored with these endless conversations which did not include her. She wondered how it was possible to have such interesting lives – advising princes, fighting battles – and to be so boring. She looked at Mrs Crawford and Mrs Minnies; they were so ugly in their dull dresses! She looked at Mr Crawford and Major Minnies, so fat and red-faced and pleased with themselves! Then she looked at her husband Douglas. At least he was different. How handsome he was in his evening clothes!

She was not the only one looking at Douglas. Harry something, who was sitting next to her, whispered to her, 'I like your husband.'

'Oh do you?' Olivia said. 'So do I.'

Harry laughed quietly and went on, 'He's so different from our other friends,' looking at the Crawfords and the Minnies. Olivia smiled back at him. Of course she agreed with him. It was nice to find someone who thought the same as she did. She had not so far met anyone in India who did. Not even, she sometimes thought, her husband.

The Nawab seemed to be listening with interest to Major Minnies, and laughed loudly at the end of the Major's story. But Olivia thought he was pretending to be amused. He was, in fact, watching his guests carefully. She would have loved to know what he thought of them all, but she was sure he would never tell her. Unless of course she got to know him really well. He often looked at her, and she pretended not to notice. She liked it. She had liked the way he had looked at her when she had first come in. For a moment his eyes had shone, then he had looked away, but

The Nawab watched his guests carefully. Olivia would have loved to know what he was thinking.

she had noticed, and realized that here at last was one person in India who was interested in her.

After this party, Olivia felt better about being alone in the house all day. She knew the Nawab would come and visit her, so every day she wore a cool, pretty dress and waited. Douglas always got up very early – very quietly so that he did not wake her – to ride to work before it got too hot. By the time Olivia woke up, the Indian servants had cleaned the house and closed all the shutters, to keep out the heat. She could do whatever she liked all day. In London she loved doing things alone for hours, but here she was beginning to hate the lonely days in the cool dark house, with silent servants waiting to serve her.

The Nawab came four days after the party. Olivia was playing the piano and went on playing, even after she had heard his car. The servant brought him in, and she turned from the piano with wide open eyes, saying, 'Oh Nawab Sahib, what a lovely surprise!'

He had come with his friend Harry, and with some young Indian men from the Palace. They stayed all day in Olivia's sitting room. Harry said he loved her room and her furniture. The Nawab clearly liked being there too. The time passed quickly. Harry talked, and Olivia and the Nawab laughed at amusing things he said. The Nawab sat in the middle of a sofa with his arms stretched out along the back, and his long legs stretched out in front. He looked handsome and relaxed and completely in control of the situation, which of course he was.

Usually when Douglas came home he found Olivia crying with tiredness and complaining that she was bored. But that evening she was so excited that at first he was afraid she was ill. When he heard about her visitor, he had a moment's doubt, but she was so happy that he decided it was all right. She was lonely, and it was kind of the Nawab to visit her.

Olivia turned from the piano with wide open eyes, saying, 'Oh Nawab Sahib, what a lovely surprise!'

A few days later another invitation arrived from the Palace for them both. The Nawab wrote that he would of course send a car to collect them. Douglas did not understand. He said the Crawfords would take them in their car as usual.

'Oh Douglas darling,' Olivia said impatiently, 'you don't think the Nawab has invited *them*, do you?' Douglas stared at her in great surprise.

Later, when it was clear that the Crawfords had really not been invited, he said he did not think he and Olivia could accept the invitation. A British official should not be too friendly with one particular Indian prince. And if Mr Crawford, the chief British official, had not been invited, then he, Douglas, who was only the assistant official, ought not to go.

But Olivia insisted, she was determined. 'I never see anyone here apart from the Crawfords, the Minnies and the Saunders,' she said. 'You know, darling, how bored I get sometimes. I *can't* miss the chance of a dinner party with some different people.'

They argued about it all day and some of the night, and in the morning Olivia even got up early to go on arguing. 'Oh Douglas, *please*,' she said, looking up at him as he sat on his horse, ready to go to work. He could not answer her because he could not promise her anything, but he wanted to, very much. He watched her walk slowly and sadly back into the house. She looked small and unhappy. 'I must be kind to her,' he thought. But he knew his duty, and that day he wrote to the Nawab, politely refusing the invitation.

Diary 28 February

I meet Chid and hear his story

The Saunders' house is now the travellers' rest-house; an old man looks after it and opens it up for people. Yesterday I met a traveller waiting for the old man to unlock it, and I started talking to him. I could tell he was English but he said his name and nationality, even his clothes, were not important to him any longer. He wore a simple orange robe, and had shaved his head completely, leaving only a little hair on top. He wanted to be like the Hindu religious men, who travel around India with no money and sometimes no clothes, and who beg for food and somewhere to sleep. He explained that he had studied Hindu religion in England, and had come to India to experience it. He had found what he was looking for in the great temples of the south, and had lived there for months, thinking only of religion. He had often been ill, but did not care. People had stolen his money and his clothes, but he did not care. He thought only of religion. He found a guru to teach him, and was given an Indian name, Chidananda (or Chid). His guru had told him to travel across India, begging for food on the way. The only thing he owned was his food bowl. Sometimes he could not get enough food, so he often had to write to his family to ask for money. And, although his guru had told him to sleep under trees, he often found this too uncomfortable and tried to find a cheap hotel room. What he hated most was the children, who ran after him and laughed at him and sometimes even threw stones at him.

At last the old man opened the rest-house. Inside it was dark and dirty. The place smelt of death. Behind the house was the Christian graveyard. In the graveyard, near the house, there was an old broken statue over a baby's grave. It was the stone angel that the Saunders had ordered from Italy for their baby's grave. I suddenly realized that Mrs Saunders had a perfect view, from the back of her house, of her baby's grave.

1923
Olivia discovers more about the Nawab

In 1923 the newest grave belonged to the Saunders' baby; it was the brightest and cleanest in the graveyard. The first time Olivia saw this baby's grave, she was very upset. When he came home, Douglas found her crying in their bedroom. 'Oh Douglas,' she said, 'what will happen if we have a baby? Perhaps it will die!'

That night Douglas had to spend the whole evening talking gently to her, and holding her. He told her that nowadays babies did not die so often. He himself had been born in India.

'What about Mrs Saunders' baby?'

'That could happen anywhere, darling.'

'It could happen to me! I'll die. We'll both die, the baby and me. If we stay here, we'll die. I know it. You'll see.' But when she saw how unhappy he looked, she tried to smile. She touched his face. 'But you want to stay,' she said.

'It's difficult for you because it's all new to you,' he said eagerly. 'It's easy for the rest of us, because we know what life is like in India.' He kissed her as he held her in his arms. 'I was just saying the same thing to Beth Crawford. Do you know what she said? She said she was sure someone as intelligent as you would certainly get used to life here, and would, well you know, come to love India in the end, the way we all do. Olivia? Are you asleep, darling?'

She wasn't really, but she liked lying in his arms in the moonlight. Douglas thought she was asleep, and held her even closer – he felt so happy to have her there, shining in the Indian moonlight.

But the next day Olivia was delighted when Beth Crawford asked her to go with her to visit the Nawab's mother, the Begum, at the royal Palace at Khatm. Olivia, Mrs Crawford and the Begum sat on European chairs, although Olivia would have preferred to sit on the carpet like the other Indian ladies. Conversation was impossible for Olivia as she did not speak a word of the language. She sat, secretly hoping that the Nawab would appear, and watched the door, while Mrs Crawford spoke to the Begum and her ladies in incorrect but confident Urdu. At the end of the visit Olivia whispered hopefully, 'Do we have to visit the Nawab too?' but Mrs Crawford said quickly, 'That will not be necessary at all,' and they left the Palace.

Then they visited Mrs Minnies, who lived just outside Khatm. She was very sympathetic.

'Oh poor Beth!' she said. 'Was your visit very boring?'

'Well, it's my duty to visit an important Indian lady like the Begum,' smiled Mrs Crawford. 'And it wasn't too bad.'

'Isn't the Nawab married?' asked Olivia suddenly.

There was a pause. The two older ladies had known each other for years and were thinking the same thing.

'Yes, he is,' said Mrs Crawford at last, 'but his wife doesn't live with him. She's not very well . . . mentally.'

'By the way,' said Mrs Minnies quickly, 'are you going to leave Satipur in the hot weather, Olivia? We'd love to have you with us in Simla. It's so much cooler in the hills. Although I'm not sure my husband will be able to come on holiday this year. He may have to stay in Khatm to make sure there's no trouble.'

'Trouble?' asked Olivia.

'Yes,' answered Mrs Minnies. 'Arthur is sure the Nawab is helping the gangs of robbers around Khatm. Do you remember the trouble three years ago, Beth? That was the Nawab again.'

'What happened?' asked Olivia eagerly.

'It was when he and his wife separated. Her family, the Cabobpurs, are very rich and important, and they were extremely angry with the Nawab. Arthur managed to stop any trouble or fighting.'

'Surely it wasn't the Nawab's fault?' said Olivia. 'If his wife was mentally ill, they couldn't live together.'

After another pause Mrs Crawford said, 'Well, we never really knew the whole story. The Nawab often seems to cause trouble, that's all we know. Now, Olivia, do say you will come away from the heat and join us in Simla, even if Douglas can't come.'

'I don't really want to leave him,' said Olivia. 'We haven't been together very long, you know,' she added shyly.

'Don't be silly, Olivia, men usually stay here and work, but we women don't have to. I know Douglas wants you to escape from the heat.'

Later that week Olivia had a visit from Harry, and she was able to get answers to some of her questions.

'What about the Nawab's wife?' she asked him.

'Ah poor Sandy. The Nawab was too much for her. He's a very strong person. When he wants something, he must have it. Her family didn't want him to marry her, but he wanted to, and so he did. You can't say no to him. By the way, Olivia – may I call you that? – he wants to give a party and he especially wants you and your husband to come.'

'Douglas is very busy, I'm afraid,' answered Olivia. 'Have you been a friend of the Nawab's for a long time?'

'Oh yes, since I met him in London. I want to do everything I can to make him happier. He's been so kind to me, he's so generous, you can't imagine. He wants his friends to have everything. He gives, all the time. But *I* want to give too.'

'He must like you very much.'

'Who knows? With him you just don't know. I've been staying with him for three years now. Three years, can you imagine, in a tiny village like Khatm. Sometimes he plans to take me travelling, to show me India, but at the last moment something always happens and we can't go. Usually it's the Begum who doesn't want us to go. I think the only person in the world he really loves is his mother. He hates being away from her. Of course, I understand that. I feel like that about *my* mother. She lives alone in a little London flat, you know. She wants me to come home. But if I ask him about leaving, he just sends her a wonderful present. Once she wrote to him saying, "The best present you could send me would be my Harry home again".'

'But he didn't let you go home?' asked Olivia.

Harry was silent for a moment. 'I'm not complaining,' he answered.

A few days later Douglas told Olivia that he had arranged for her to go up to the mountains with Beth Crawford and Mary Minnies during the hot weather. 'You'll love it, darling,' he said. 'The scenery is beautiful, and it's so much cooler than here.'

'I'm not going without you,' said Olivia.

'Now, Olivia, listen,' said her husband. 'All the wives go up to the hills. My mother did. Everyone does.'

'Well, I'm not going.' Olivia looked straight at him, to show that she was determined. 'By the way, the Nawab wants to give a party for us. He sent Harry to invite us.'

'Well, we can't go, that's all,' said Douglas calmly.

'But I'm so bored, Douglas!' she cried. Then as she looked into his clear honest eyes, she remembered how much she loved him. 'Darling, I'll be bored, I'll be hot, I'll be cross, but please don't send me away to the hills with the other women! I want to stay here with you!'

The next day the Nawab arrived at her house. '*I've* come to visit *you*, because you won't accept my invitation,' he said to Olivia. 'Would you like to come for a drive, and then perhaps have a picnic? Please say yes. It will only take a short time. You must come!'

It was impossible to refuse him. So Olivia, Harry and the Nawab drove out of the town and into the burning heat and dust.

'Oh Douglas, please don't send me away to the hills with the other women! I want to stay here with you!'

The Nawab sat next to her, relaxed and silent, with one arm stretched along the back of the seat, and smoked cigarette after cigarette. No one said where they were going. This was all the Nawab's land and Olivia felt helpless. The Nawab's silence upset her. Was he bored, or angry? Then the car stopped, and they got out and walked up a steep narrow path. Still nobody spoke. Olivia did not know why she was there and she felt hot and tired and near to tears. At last they arrived at a stone shrine. It was cool and green here, with trees and a stream. The palace servants had arrived earlier, and were preparing food and drinks. There were carpets and cushions to lie on.

Now the Nawab became polite and interested again. 'I'm so sorry you felt hot in the car. What a terrible climate we have!'

'It's lovely here,' said Olivia gratefully. She felt cooler, and was happy now that he was being nice to her again.

'It's a very special place. Come and see it with me,' he said.

The shrine was a small white building. Inside there were dying flowers on the ground. 'It's a religious place,' he explained. 'People come here to ask God for help. I'll tell you why it was built. One of my family, Amanullah Khan, who lived a long time ago, was hurt in a fight with his enemies and escaped to this place. Baba Firdaus, a good Hindu who used to live here, hid him and looked after him. Many years later, Amanullah Khan came back to thank Baba Firdaus, but the old man had gone away or died, so Amanullah Khan built this shrine. It was the only way he could thank the old man who had saved his life. He never forgot a friend or an enemy,' finished the Nawab. 'You British like people like that.'

Olivia laughed. Together they walked to the stream.

'You see,' said the Nawab, 'in the middle of this desert there is water. Is it a miracle? Is it because Baba Firdaus was such a good man? Or is it because Amanullah Khan remembered to come back to thank his friend?' He knelt down, put his fingers in the water and invited Olivia to do the same. They were side by side. The Nawab looked at her closely. 'What do you think? Is it a miracle?'

Olivia looked at the stream. It was very shallow, with only a little water in it. 'I think,' she said, 'it is a very *small* miracle.'

The Nawab laughed loudly. 'Oh Mrs Rivers!' he shouted. 'You have a good sense of humour! Do you know, as soon as I saw you,

I thought we would get on well together. I feel I can say anything to you, and you will understand. You and I are much more alike than, for example, Mrs Crawford.' They both laughed. He looked into her eyes. 'You are not at all like Mrs Crawford.'

They went back to Harry and the servants, and the picnic lasted all day. The Nawab was in a very cheerful mood, and Olivia had never enjoyed herself so much.

Diary 8 March

I discover more about Inder Lal

I see from Olivia's letters that she only really started writing long letters to her sister Marcia after the day of the Nawab's picnic. Olivia didn't tell Douglas about the picnic, because he was so busy and did not have much time to talk or listen to her, so she wrote to her sister about it.

I have put Olivia's letters on my little desk and I work on them and my diary every morning. My day in Satipur starts early, when I hear the temple bells. I buy vegetables at the market, cook breakfast, then work at my desk. In the evening I go to the Post Office (which is in what used to be the breakfast-room of Olivia's house). Sometimes I wait for my landlord Inder Lal to finish work at his office in the Crawfords' old house, and we walk home together. He quite likes practising his English, and even discussing personal feelings with me.

'I cannot discuss feelings with my wife,' he said once. 'She is not intelligent.' I remembered his wife Ritu's face, thin, tired and miserable. We walked past some boys swimming in the lake. They were shouting and laughing. Inder Lal looked sadly at them. Perhaps he wished he had never married, and was free to enjoy

Sometimes I wait for my landlord Inder Lal to finish work, and we walk home together.

himself with his friends again. Sometimes he looks old and tired, but I know he is young, only 25 or 26, younger than me in fact. His eyes are beautiful – full of sadness and feeling.

Diary 10 March

I begin to get used to India

I'm working hard at learning Hindi, and can now have conversations with people. I try to talk to Ritu, but she is so shy that she sometimes runs away and hides in the bathroom if she sees me coming!

It's really hot here now, even at night. Everyone sleeps outside, in the streets and gardens. Even I do. It's surprising how quiet everything is at night. I lie awake for hours, so happy. Lying on my bed outside, I feel I am close to the sky, but not alone, because there are hundreds of people sleeping around me. I feel I am part of India.

Diary 20 March

I make Indian friends and meet Maji

Inder Lal's mother and I have become good friends. She comes with me to market and helps me to buy the best vegetables. We talk together in Hindi. I like listening when she tells me about herself. Although her husband is dead, she says the best part of her life is now. She says that when an Indian girl marries, she has to live with her husband's family, and it's difficult to get used to them. So now she is free, she spends a lot of time with other women friends, laughing and talking and going out.

Sometimes she invites me to come too. I've met an important member of her group of friends, called Maji. They say she is a holy woman who can do things which ordinary people can't (I don't know if it's magic or miracles), and she lives in a little house near the lake. I really like being with these older Indian women – they seem so happy, cheerful and relaxed.

In India dead bodies are burned, and it was an ancient custom for a widow to be burnt alive with her husband's body. Inder Lal's mother showed me the local shrines to these brave wives. The British forbade the custom, and the last shrine is dated 1923.

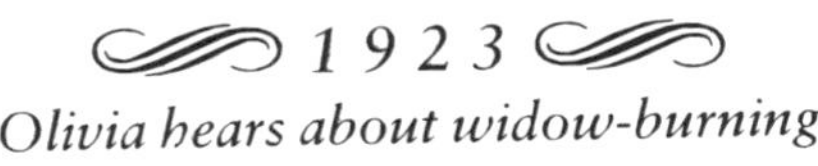

1923

Olivia hears about widow-burning

It happened when Mr Crawford was away on business and Douglas was in control of the district. A woman was forced by her family to burn herself with her husband's dead body. Douglas arrived too late to stop the burning, but he calmly arrested her relations for breaking the law.

Since the picnic, the Nawab had visited Olivia several times, but she had still not told her husband either about the picnic or the Nawab's frequent visits. Of course she wanted to tell him, but he was so busy that she never seemed to have the chance. On the day of the burning, however, the Nawab did not leave until after Douglas arrived home. The Nawab greeted Douglas warmly and congratulated him on arresting the dead woman's family.

Douglas said coldly, 'Thank you, but I only wish I could have prevented her death.'

'What can be done, Mr Rivers?' said the Nawab sympathetically. 'These people will never learn. But Mr Rivers, everyone must be grateful to you for acting strongly. And you, Mrs Rivers,' he added, turning to Olivia, 'you need never worry. Where Mr Rivers is, there is firm control. These people need it.'

The other British officials also congratulated Douglas, who was secretly delighted. At a dinner party at the Crawfords', they all discussed the forbidden custom.

'Those poor women!' said Mrs Minnies. 'Forced to die in such a terrible way!'

'Well,' said her husband, 'some wives really wanted to die with their husbands, you know.'

'I don't believe it!' said Dr Saunders.

'The latest one didn't want to die,' said Douglas quietly. He could remember very clearly the woman's screams, but he had not told Olivia about them.

'How do you know?' Olivia challenged him. She wanted to know more about it. 'Surely it's part of their religion, isn't it? Perhaps we should let them keep these ancient customs, if they want to.' She did not really support widow-burning, but she felt angry with the others – they were smiling and interested, but they were so *sure* they knew best.

'But it's very brave, isn't it?' she went on, not daring to look at Douglas. She knew he was looking coldly at her. 'I mean, wanting to die when the person you love most in the world is dead.'

Beth Crawford felt the conversation was becoming too serious. 'Too brave for me, I'm afraid,' she laughed. 'I'm sure I couldn't. . .'

'Oh I could!' cried Olivia, with such feeling that everyone looked at her. 'I'd be *grateful* for a custom like that.' She had to look at Douglas. Was he angry with her for disagreeing with the others? But the cold look in his eyes turned into love as their eyes met. At that moment Olivia loved him so much that she could not go on looking into his eyes. She looked down at her plate and went on eating, thinking that everything was all right as long as she and Douglas loved each other.

Diary 30 March

I take Chid home with me

One day when Inder Lal and I were walking home from his office, we heard strange cries near the lake. When I went to look, I found the man in the orange robe, Chid, who had talked to me outside the travellers' rest-house. He was lying in a cave, and looked very ill.

'I don't know how long I've been ill,' he told me, 'and I'm hungry and thirsty,' he added.

'Who is he?' whispered Inder Lal, who didn't want to get too close.

'I met him some time ago. He's been studying Indian religion.' Inder Lal was very interested in this.

'I have nowhere to go, and I'm still very ill,' said Chid. 'Do you live near here? I think I could walk there if it's *very* near.'

'Well . . .' I answered. I was not enthusiastic.

But Inder Lal said eagerly, 'What a good idea, yes, it's very near.' So we took Chid home with us.

Diary 10 April

I have to look after Chid

Chid's illness disappeared after a few days, but he has shown no sign of leaving. I suppose it's restful for him in my room after all his travelling across India. It's not very restful for me, though. He's always hungry and eats all the food I cook for him. But I don't like the way he takes anything he wants. He tells me he doesn't believe in things belonging to people – everything should be shared. He even shares my body! And he wants to make love very often. However, my Indian friends think I am very fortunate to have this chance of serving a good man. I'm not sure whether Chid is good or not, but Indians believe he is, just because he has shaved his head and thrown away his clothes. Indians are very kind to all beggars and religious men.

As soon as Inder Lal comes home from work, he climbs upstairs to my room and sits for hours listening to Chid talking about religion. I find it very boring. It seems to me that Chid doesn't know much about it. Sometimes he seems a bit mad.

I suppose it's restful for Chid in my room after all his travelling across India.

Diary 15 April

My friends and I visit the shrine

Things often get confused in India. An example of this is the story of Baba Firdaus' shrine. The Nawab had explained to Olivia how it had been built by Amanullah Khan, a Muslim. Now, in this century, the shrine is visited on one day a year by Hindu women who want babies and have not yet had any. There are many stories about why the shrine is holy. Some people say that a childless woman had been sent away from her husband's house, so that he could marry again. On the day of her husband's second wedding she came to the shrine to hide her sadness, and here she had a dream that she would have a baby in nine months' time.

And so she did. This festival is called the Husband's Wedding Day. However, there are many other stories about the shrine, so we can't easily discover which one is correct.

Yesterday was the Husband's Wedding Day, and I went with Inder Lal's mother and her women friends to the shrine. The bus was full of women all going to the same place, laughing, shouting, and enjoying their day out. The Nawab's favourite picnic place has changed a lot! Now there are games, and people selling food, and crowds of visitors.

We found a quiet place under a shady tree and ate our picnic, sharing our food. I enjoyed listening to the women's stories. Then they turned to me and asked, 'What about you? What do you want from the shrine?' I laughed and said they had brought me to the wrong shrine – first I needed a husband, not a baby. They all laughed at this, but I could see that they thought it was a serious problem.

Yesterday was the Husband's Wedding Day, and I went with Inder Lal's mother and her women friends to the shrine.

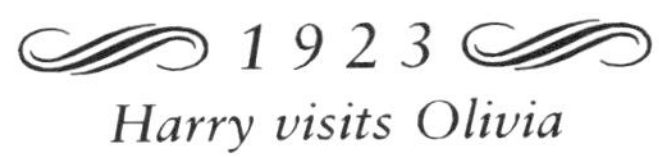

1923
Harry visits Olivia

The Husband's Wedding Day was always a difficult time for Major Minnies. Fighting often broke out between Muslims and Hindus around Baba Firdaus' shrine. In those days there were still a lot of Muslims in Khatm (when India became independent in 1947, some were killed and others ran away to Pakistan). The Nawab himself was a Muslim. Many of the Muslims did not like the Hindus using a Muslim shrine for a Hindu festival, and the shrine was on the Nawab's land. Major Minnies was not allowed to give orders, but he tried giving advice to the Nawab, who used to laugh kindly at him and say, 'My dear Major, of course, just as you say, why do you worry?'

But nothing was done, and so in that first summer of Olivia's, there was fighting in Khatm on the Husband's Wedding Day. Olivia herself did not notice anything. She was in her cool elegant house, playing the piano. All the doors and windows were shut because there was so much dust blowing about outside in the hot wind. Although she did not know about the violence in Khatm, she knew Douglas was worried that there might be trouble even in Satipur, which was usually so quiet.

Later that morning Mrs Crawford and Mrs Minnies came to visit her. 'Don't worry, Olivia,' said Mrs Crawford. 'There won't be any fighting here. My husband and yours can control the people.'

'But Khatm is quite different,' said Mrs Minnies. 'Remember last year, Beth? Twelve people killed and seventy-five hurt. And Arthur warned the Nawab again and again – but he did nothing. It may be worse this year.'

'It's very bad,' said Mrs Crawford, shaking her head. 'He could easily stop the violence if he wanted to . . .'

'The Nawab?' asked Olivia. 'But of course he wants to!'

'Don't forget he's a Muslim too, so he doesn't like the Hindus,' they told her.

'Yes, but he doesn't feel strongly about religion.' She laughed at the idea. 'He's such a modern person. Almost like one of us. I mean, when we were talking about widow-burning, he sounded just like an English person. He said it was an awful old custom.'

'Of course he would say that,' answered Mrs Crawford. 'He doesn't like widow-burning because it's a Hindu custom.'

Olivia did not believe them, but she could not argue with them. It was always like that. They believed they alone knew the real India. But this time she felt *she* knew the Nawab and they did not. To them he was just another Indian prince, but to her he was – well, he was a friend.

Some time after they had gone, she heard a car outside. The Nawab! She felt her heart beating loudly, and she rushed to the door. But from the car a voice cried, 'It's me!' It was the Nawab's car, but it was Harry who stepped out. Clouds of hot dust blew into her sitting room as he came in. He looked hot and exhausted.

'What's happening in Khatm?' she asked him immediately.

Harry lay back in an armchair with his eyes closed. 'Don't ask me, I don't know,' he replied tiredly. 'I live at the Palace, remember, and there's no trouble there. I stayed in my room all day yesterday and this morning. What else can you do in this terrible heat? Have you *seen* what it's like outside? These dust storms go on for ever, you know. Sometimes people go mad in the heat.' He stopped himself and was silent for a moment, then he went on, 'I think I nearly went mad myself. There I was, locked up in my room, imagining the fighting outside. It was the same last year, and the one before. But at least this year I've got someone to talk to about it. Dear Olivia! I didn't see any fighting on my way here, you know, but I heard a lot of shouting. When I asked the Nawab if it would be safe to drive through Khatm to get here, he said, "Of course you will be safe in *my* car!" and thought that was a great joke. He's strange at the moment. He seems very excited and he laughs a lot. He seems to be waiting for something.' Harry closed his eyes again and did not talk any more.

When Douglas came home, he invited Harry to stay with them for a few days, and sent the Nawab's car back. Harry was delighted, and he and Olivia spent the next two days singing, playing the piano and reading in Olivia's beautiful sitting room, while the dust and the wind blew wildly outside the house.

One day Mrs Crawford came to visit them. 'Olivia,' she said, 'you really must join us in the mountains during the hot weather. Don't you agree, Harry?'

'Yes, I do,' he said. 'It's awful here when it's really hot, Olivia. You should go with them, you know.'

'But *you* stay here in the hot weather!' she replied.

'I do, but I don't like it!' He had spoken quickly, then was sorry he had shown his feelings and tried to make a joke of it. 'Of course, we at the Palace have a thousand plans to leave immediately for the mountains. We're always packing and unpacking.' He laughed but his voice was shaking. 'Something always goes wrong at the last minute, so in the end we stay at home. The Begum doesn't really want to go, you see. I've got used to it now, like everyone else at the Palace.' Suddenly he turned to Mrs Crawford and spoke quickly. 'My mother keeps writing and asking me to come – she's not well and I'm worried about her. She lives alone in a flat, and I've been away for three years now.'

'That *is* a long time,' said Mrs Crawford.

'I was only going to stay for six months, but whenever I talk about going home, he doesn't like it. He hates people leaving him. He loves his friends so much, you see. He has such a warm heart.' He looked down at the floor.

After a while Mrs Crawford said brightly, 'Some friends of ours are going home to England soon. They're coming to stay with us, and then they're driving to Bombay to catch their ship. Perhaps you could go with them?'

She looked at Harry. His eyes were shining. 'Do you think I could get a ticket?' he asked eagerly. 'I mean, perhaps all the places on the ship are reserved already.'

'Oh, that's no problem for one person,' answered Mrs Crawford. 'A friend of mine in Bombay could get you a ticket.'

'Really?' Harry said, so full of glad hope that she smiled.

'Really,' she promised him.

That night Olivia asked Douglas anxiously, 'Do you think it's all right for Harry to go home, darling?'

'Of course,' said her husband, 'he *wants* to go.'

'But the Nawab invited him here, and . . . has been very generous and kind to him . . . and doesn't want him to go!'

'Well, I don't care,' said Douglas. 'It's better for Harry to go home now. His mother needs him, and he's lived with Indians long enough.'

The next day Harry was still at Douglas and Olivia's. It was Sunday, and when the Rivers came back from church they found the Nawab's car outside their house. The Nawab and Harry had obviously had a long friendly conversation together, and now the Nawab said, 'Thank you so much for looking after my friend here. I am taking him back to Khatm.'

Douglas's back was straight as he looked coldly at the Nawab, who added, 'Now that everything is quiet at Khatm, he needn't be afraid,' and smiled kindly at Harry, who smiled back. Douglas said nothing. He and the Nawab were standing face to face, a stiff, angry British official and a smiling, polite Indian prince.

'Do sit down, both of you!' cried Olivia, but they did not hear her.

'Perhaps you have heard we had a little trouble in Khatm,' said the Nawab.

Douglas stared straight ahead of him, and said nothing.

'It happens every year,' said the Nawab, 'it's not important.'

'We know how many people died,' said Douglas coldly.

'We can't prevent it,' smiled the Nawab.

Douglas could not say what he thought. He had to be polite. So he stayed silent. But his silence was full of feeling.

Douglas and the Nawab were standing face to face, a stiff, angry British official and a smiling, polite Indian prince.

The Nawab turned to Harry and said, 'Come on, Harry, we're going now.'

Douglas said suddenly, 'I believe Mrs Crawford's friends are arriving tomorrow.'

'Oh yes,' said the Nawab, 'I know, they are the people driving to Bombay. Harry told me. But he's not going with them. He has decided not to go.'

Douglas said to Harry, 'Mr Crawford has booked a ticket for you on the ship, if you want to leave.'

The Nawab now sat down, looking very relaxed. 'Harry and I have talked about it,' he said. 'It was all a mistake. I'll apologize to Mr and Mrs Crawford and their friends.' He smiled at Olivia.

Again Douglas spoke directly to Harry. 'You wanted to go. Your mother's ill.'

Again the Nawab replied. 'Fortunately, Harry's mother is better now. And we have invited her to stay at the Palace. We are very much looking forward to her visit. My mother herself has written to invite her.' He smiled at everybody, pleased with his family's correct behaviour.

At last Harry spoke. 'Thanks for everything,' he said to Douglas. 'It's true, you know, I do want to stay at the Palace.'

'You don't have to,' Douglas told him.

'No, but I want to,' answered Harry.

The Nawab started laughing. 'You see, Mr and Mrs Rivers, he is just like a child! We others have to decide everything for him. Now, please get ready to leave, Harry.' When Harry left the room, the Nawab turned to Douglas and Olivia, saying seriously, 'Sometimes, you know, Harry is rather selfish. But what can I do? I've become fond of him, and he has his place here.' The Nawab laid his hand on his heart.

Such a strong friendship, thought Olivia, such a deep love, and all for Harry! She believed every word the Nawab said. But Douglas went on staring coldly at the Indian until he and Harry left the house.

Diary 25 April

I want Chid to leave

Chid and I are part of the town now. Indian people here accept us, as they accept the beggars. There are a lot of beggars in Satipur, some of them ill, some blind, and some who can't walk. I've got used to them now, but I hated seeing them at first.

Dust storms have started blowing all day and all night. Hot winds whistle clouds of dust out of the desert into the town. There is dust everywhere – in the air, in the trees. Everyone is cross, restless, uncomfortable. But Chid doesn't notice the weather. He sits quietly in a corner of my room, meditating for hours. He never seems to do anything – it makes me angry. He often wants to make love, but it's too hot, so I refuse. Anyway, he's dirty – bathing is one Hindu custom he doesn't practise. And as he doesn't believe people should own things, he often takes my money, so now I have to hide it.

Today I was so angry with him that I threw his things down the stairs. 'Go away!' I shouted. 'You can't stay here!'

But he just collected his things and brought them back upstairs to my room. Then he sat down on the floor and began meditating again.

'You can't stay!' I shouted again. But when he's meditating he doesn't hear anyone, and he seems to be in another world. He moves his lips and his eyes stare at nothing. He looks so happy.

Diary 30 April

Ritu's illness

Inder Lal's wife Ritu seems to be ill, mentally ill. Sometimes she doesn't listen or seem to hear when you speak to her. Sometimes she starts screaming for no reason at all. The hot weather makes her worse, so now she is kept locked up in a room. Our neighbours have got used to her screams and hardly notice the noise any more, but I hate hearing her crying.

'She ought to have medical help,' I told Chid one day. 'She needs treatment.'

'Today she's going to have some,' he answered. 'A man is coming to make her better.'

That day we heard the screams again, but this time they were completely different. They sounded like an animal in terrible pain. Even our neighbours stopped to listen. But Chid remained calm. 'It's just her treatment,' he said. 'They get rid of the evil spirit inside her body, by burning her arms or feet. It's an old custom here.'

Next day I went to meet Inder Lal outside his office. I had decided to speak to him about modern treatment of mental illness. 'It's a kind of science,' I explained. This made him very interested; he is always eager to learn about anything new. But when I spoke about the kind of treatment they had given Ritu, he looked away and said unhappily, 'I don't believe in that kind of treatment.'

'So why did you agree to it?'

'My mother's friends all advised this treatment, and my mother thought we should try it, because we've tried every other way of helping Ritu, and she's still ill.'

We walked the rest of the way home in silence.

Diary 2 May

A pilgrimage is planned

I suggested modern treatment for Ritu's illness, but Maji, the holy woman and friend of the family, has suggested a pilgrimage. One day she explained to me, 'If someone is very unhappy or mentally ill, then they go on a long, long journey right up into the highest mountains in the world, the Himalayas. It is a beautiful and holy experience. When Ritu comes back, she will be well and happy.'

So Inder Lal's mother and Ritu are leaving in a few days' time, and Chid is going with them! I am delighted about that. I wonder if Maji has persuaded him to go because she knows I want to get rid of him? Of course I've never complained to her about Chid, but she seems to know most things without being told. She is a fat, cheerful woman, and every time she looks at Chid, she gives a shout of laughter. 'Good boy!' she cries – perhaps the only two words of English she knows.

She went on explaining to me, 'All kinds of people go on the pilgrimage, from all over India. They travel for months away from their homes to get there. On the way they stop at temples and rest-houses. At last they reach the mountains and begin to climb. Ah, those mountains!' cried Maji. 'Yes, it's like climbing into heaven. There is cool fresh air, clouds, birds and trees. Then there is only snow, and everything is shining white. They come close to the shrine at the top of the mountain. Some people fall down with happiness. All of them shout the holy name of God!'

'I will too!' cried Chid excitedly.

'Good boy! Good boy!' she said, encouraging him.

I must say, sitting here in the dust storm under the hot yellow sky, I wanted to be in the cool air of those snowy mountains myself.

1923
Olivia becomes more friendly with the Nawab

The other British women had left Satipur and gone up to the mountains to escape the heat. Although Douglas had tried to persuade Olivia to go with them, now he was glad she had stayed. They spent lovely evenings and nights together. Olivia understood that, when he came home, Douglas wanted to relax with her in their elegant house, and forget the heat and problems of the day. So she was always cheerful and careful not to worry him. She never talked about the Nawab, for example. That would upset him. Douglas loved her more than ever, but he found it difficult to express his love.

During the day Olivia usually went to the Palace. Harry came in one of the Nawab's cars to collect her, and together they drove to Khatm. Now she was even beginning to enjoy these morning drives. The huge sky, the clouds of dust and the burning sun outside the car made her feel she was in a different world, not part of the real world at all.

They usually spent the day drinking, smoking, playing cards and talking. One day the Nawab said, 'Olivia,' (he called her Olivia now) 'you play the piano so beautifully but you have never played mine.'

'Where is it?' she asked, looking round the great hall they were sitting in. There were expensive sofas, armchairs and tables, but no piano.

'Come, I will show you,' he laughed. He led her through empty rooms and dark passages to an underground room, which contained all kinds of games, furniture and equipment. These things had been ordered from Europe some time in the past, but had

Douglas loved Olivia more than ever, but he found it difficult to express his love.

never been used and were now covered in dust. There were also two pianos.

'You see? My pianos,' said the Nawab proudly. Olivia sat down at the larger one and tried to play it, but it was in such bad condition that it produced a terrible sound.

'Oh, what a pity,' she said. She really meant it.

'Yes,' he replied, 'you're right.' He too was suddenly sad. He sat down heavily on a dusty box. After a short silence he said, 'They were ordered for my wife.'

Olivia tried again, but the sounds were too heart-breaking.

'Can it be mended?' he asked eagerly.

'Oh yes, there's a man in Bombay who can do it. I'd like him to work on my piano too. But Bombay is so far away!'

'Why didn't you tell me before? In future you must tell me if there is anything I can do for you. I will send for him, and he can mend your piano and mine. By the way, did you know I was married?'

'I've heard,' said Olivia quietly.

'What have you heard?' he asked sharply, looking closely into her face. She did not answer. 'You will hear many things about me. People are always ready to tell lies. But – the pianos, Olivia. If they are repaired and I bring them upstairs, will you play them for me? It will make me so very happy. Sandy, my wife, you know, wanted to learn the piano, so I sent for them, but by the time they arrived, she had gone away. Please play for me now.'

'But it sounds so awful.'

'Play for me.'

Olivia played as well as she could, but the sounds that came out were strange and unpleasant. It was extraordinary, but the Nawab seemed to like it, and went on, 'I miss Sandy very much. She was a modern girl, you know, not like the Indian ladies. She was like you, Olivia. And she was beautiful, like you.' He spoke sadly and suddenly turned to leave the room. Although Olivia was in the middle of playing, she had to hurry after him because she knew she could not find her way back through the dark passages without him.

It was about this time, the time of her growing friendship with the Nawab, that she and Douglas began to talk seriously about having children. They both wanted children very much. Olivia said that someone as handsome, as perfect as Douglas, should have many sons all exactly like him. Not at all, he said; it was daughters like Olivia he wanted – as many of them as possible. Lovingly, he kissed his wife's shoulder.

'Of course we'll stay in India with our children, and then they'll get jobs here,' said Olivia, 'in the army perhaps, or in politics. But darling,' – she had a moment's doubt – 'you don't think things will ever change in India, do you? I mean, perhaps we British will have to leave one day and the Indians will become independent?'

Douglas smiled calmly at her. 'Don't worry, darling,' he said confidently, 'they will need us for a long time. They can't manage without us.'

That evening Olivia gave a dinner party for Mr Crawford and Major Minnies. She told the servants to carry the table into the garden, where it was cooler. They sat eating in the moonlight.

'No holiday for you, Minnies?' asked Mr Crawford sympathetically. 'You're still having trouble with the Nawab, are you?'

'Is it still that awful Husband's Wedding Day problem?' asked Olivia shyly.

'No, no,' answered the Major. 'That wasn't too bad this year. Only six killed and forty-three hurt. No, the present problem involves these gangs of robbers. I think the Nawab will be in serious trouble soon.'

'What kind of trouble?' asked Olivia.

'Well, the British government don't like it if an Indian prince becomes the leader of a gang of robbers.'

'The leader!' cried Olivia. Her voice sounded really shocked, and she looked quickly at Douglas, but he had not noticed.

'Of course we all know he owes a lot of money. But we've now discovered that he is organizing gangs to go out and attack and rob people. I have to put this information in my regular reports to the government, so one day he will be punished.'

The men were all silent, too angry to speak.

'Indian princes often make stupid mistakes,' continued the Major. 'I've known a lot of them while I've been in India. Sometimes it's because they're stupid. But it's worse when they're not.

Like the Nawab. He has everything, he's handsome, intelligent and educated. It's sad to see him becoming . . . What is it, dear lady? Are you leaving us?'

'Yes, to your drinks and cigars,' said Olivia.

They all stood up politely as she walked through the moonlight to the house. Then they sat down again and went on drinking and smoking.

Olivia went upstairs but she did not want to go to bed yet. She looked out of her bedroom window into the garden, where she could see the three men still sitting round the table. Probably now that she had gone they were talking more freely – about the Nawab and his bad behaviour. She felt strange, strange. She looked beyond the three Englishmen in their evening clothes in her garden, with the servants all waiting near the table in case they were needed. In the distance she could see the Saunders' house in the moonlight, and then the little church and the graveyard, and beyond that the flat scenery which she knew so well, those miles of brown earth that led to Khatm.

Diary 12 June

I remember Karim and Kitty

I keep getting letters from Chid on his pilgrimage. I was surprised to receive the first one, as I didn't think he was the kind of person to remember a friend. He always writes the same kind of letter – a lot of talk about religion with a few lines of information in the middle, and at the end a request. I keep his letters on my desk with Olivia's. It's interesting to compare them. Olivia's letters are about her life; she wrote beautifully but very fast, just as she thought or felt. However, Chid's letters are not about himself at all, but about

God. His letters, only a few days old, look ancient and dirty; they even smell of India. But Olivia's still look fresh and clean, and they smell of perfume.

Inder Lal is always eager to hear Chid's letters. He comes up to my room in the evenings so that I can read them out to him. He likes all that talk of religion. He tells me that Chid's spirit is a very old one, which in the past has lived in many different bodies. He thinks most of these bodies belonged to Indians, and that's why Chid has come back to India in this life. But what Inder Lal doesn't understand is why *I* have come. He doesn't think *my* spirit has ever lived in an Indian body, so why have I come to India in this life? I try to think of a reason. I tell him that many Europeans are tired of the West and its rich people, and we come to India hoping to find a simpler and more natural way of life. Most of us are not even religious, but we are looking for peace. This explanation offends Inder Lal. He can't understand it, and thinks I am laughing at Indians.

'Why should people like you who have everything – cars, fridges and so on – come to a place like India where there is nothing?' he asks. 'When you're here, I feel ashamed of my poor food and my tiny house,' he adds.

I try to protest, but he goes on rather wildly, 'I'm not surprised you laugh at us! We have nothing here! And as for me, I know nothing about the modern world! Laugh, go on! Yes, you should laugh! You know, I often feel I want to laugh myself when I see the terrible conditions people live in. For example,' he cries, pointing out of the window at a beggar in the street, 'you see him, he can't walk. He makes you laugh, doesn't he!'

When he talks like this, I remember Karim and Kitty. I had visited them in London just before coming to India. Karim is the Nawab's nephew, who inherited the Palace, and Kitty, his wife, is also the daughter of an Indian prince. When I telephoned Karim and told him I was going to India to find out more about the Nawab and Khatm, he invited me to his London flat. He himself opened the door. He was a very handsome young man, and he and his wife both wore elegant London clothes.

The sitting room was full of their Indian friends, who were sitting on the carpets and on brightly coloured sofas. But there were also two English people there, who told me that they were going to start a business with Karim and Kitty, making clothes out of Indian materials.

Karim sat on a cushion at my feet and looked up at me with his beautiful eyes. 'You must tell me what you want to find out in India,' he said.

'Well, I'm specially interested in your uncle, the Nawab,' I replied.

'Ah, wasn't he a bad boy?' he said, and everyone laughed.

'There were a lot of bad boys in those days,' someone said.

I realized that all these Indians were from royal families, as they began to tell stories of the past, when the British controlled India.

'My grandfather was involved in a scandal in a London hotel,' said someone else.

'Well, do you remember my uncle?' asked a third. 'He spent all the family fortune on himself.'

'What about my father?' said a fourth. 'The British removed him from his palace because he behaved badly.'

'My uncle poisoned my father, so that he would inherit the money and become prince,' said another.

They all agreed that it had been a most exciting time, and seemed quite sad that it was all over.

Then they started discussing modern India, which sounded much less exciting.

'India is, of course, home,' said Karim, 'but it's becoming so impossible to live there that we have to stay in England most of the time.'

'I mean, we want to do what we can to help India,' one of his friends said, 'but the Indian government really is making things very difficult for us.'

'That's right,' they all agreed.

'For example,' said one girl, 'my family tried to interest a foreign company in our palace. We thought it could become a hotel. It needed new bathrooms, of course. But the Indian government kept on refusing to give permission, so in the end the foreign company lost interest in the plan. Now our palace is empty, with a broken roof. We had to sell all the furniture. It's very sad.'

'We had to sell most of the things from the Palace at Khatm too,' Karim told me. 'But there are a few pictures in the next room, which I kept to remind me of the family. Come. I'll show you.' He jumped up, stretching his long legs, and led me into another sitting room. There were pictures of princes and their wives, all wearing expensive jewels.

'Unfortunately, most of the family jewels disappeared a long time ago,' said Karim. 'In fact,' he added, smiling, 'it was my uncle the Nawab who sold them. He always needed money and he didn't care how he got it. Oh yes, he was involved in many scandals, even – perhaps you've heard? – with an Englishwoman. She was the wife of a British official in Satipur.'

'Yes,' I said, and walked on to look at the next picture.

'Ah yes,' said Karim, 'this is a very important member of my family, Amanullah Khan.' I remembered that he was the one whose life was saved by Baba Firdaus. Karim seemed as proud of him as the Nawab had always been.

'He was a brave man when he was fighting his enemies. But sometimes he got very angry, especially while he was drinking.

Once in an argument he cut off a man's arm! Just like that! What a man! Mine is an old family, and we've been Nawabs since 1817. I could go back to India, join the government perhaps. I do want to serve my country, you know, but the trouble is, every time we go to Khatm, Kitty is ill. It's because of the water. And of course there's no proper doctor there, so we always have to get back to the hotel in Bombay as quickly as possible. But now we're thinking of buying a flat in Bombay when we start this business with our English friends. So we'll be helping India, won't we, by selling Indian materials and ideas to the West?'

He looked at me with his beautiful dark eyes (rather like Inder Lal's, I discovered later). I never met him again, and I couldn't imagine him or Kitty at Khatm or Satipur, or even Bombay.

1923

Harry is ill, and Olivia visits the graveyard

Olivia still went to the Palace in the Nawab's car almost every day, but Harry no longer came to collect her. He was not well. He said it was because of the heat or the food from the Nawab's kitchen. Although the Nawab ordered the food himself, and it was carefully prepared, Harry still did not like it.

So he stayed in his room, and Olivia visited him there. But he seemed angry with her. Once he even said to her, quite sharply, 'Douglas doesn't know you come to Khatm, does he?' and then, 'You shouldn't keep coming. You shouldn't be here.'

'That's what Douglas says about you,' answered Olivia. 'He thinks you shouldn't stay with the Nawab. But it seems to me you are quite comfortable here.'

She looked round at his beautiful room, with its antique English furniture, its Indian pictures, its windows overlooking the rose gardens.

'Have you noticed something?' Harry said. 'He never takes you to meet the Begum and her ladies.'

'I *have* met them, thank you.' She smiled stiffly. 'It wasn't easy talking to them.'

'Well, I think it's rude,' said Harry, 'to you.'

'I don't *want* to meet the Begum,' said Olivia quickly. 'I come here to be with you – and him of course – as your friend. Both of you. I can't be friends with the Begum, can I? She doesn't speak my language. I enjoy being here. We have a good time, don't we? Don't look at me like that, Harry. Now you're like everyone else. You're trying to make me feel I don't understand, that I don't know India. It's true, I don't, but that doesn't matter. We can still be friends, can't we, even if we are in India?'

She spoke in a hurry. She did not want an answer, she just wanted to show that she was right, to explain. Then she asked, 'What's all this about gangs of robbers, Harry? Tell me, please.'

Harry looked tired and replied, 'Really, I don't know, Olivia. A lot of things happen here, and I prefer not to know about them. Oh, I do feel ill. I feel awful. It's this terrible heat.'

'But it's *cool* in here. It's lovely.'

'But outside, it's so hot outside!' He shut his eyes.

She went to the window. The sun was very strong, but the Nawab's gardens looked cool and green, and the fountains shone like jewels in the bright sunlight. Beyond the pearl-grey walls of the Palace she could see the broken roofs of Khatm, and beyond that the dusty road to Satipur, where Douglas was – but why look that far? Everything was very pleasant here.

The Nawab came in quietly. 'Am I disturbing you? Please say if

I am, and I'll go away at once.' He looked anxiously at Harry, then turned to Olivia. 'What do you think about our patient? I've sent for doctors but he doesn't like them. They're Indian, of course, and he thinks they don't know anything about medicine.'

'They don't,' said Harry from his bed.

'Really, Harry,' said the Nawab, smiling kindly, 'they're perfectly good doctors. Now you must get well quickly. I miss you. It's very boring without you – isn't it, Olivia?' And he turned right round to look at her, bringing her into that warm circle of friendship.

'She's been asking about the gangs of robbers,' said Harry.

At that moment the Nawab was looking straight at Olivia. She saw a strange look in his eyes which he could not hide quickly enough. He seemed to be looking for something in her face. Then he turned away. He said quietly, 'Olivia, I hope that if you want to know something, something you don't understand, you won't ask Harry or anybody else, only me. Who has spoken to you? Who has told you these stories? Tell me, so that I can tell you the truth.'

'Do you want her to be your spy?' said Harry. 'To bring back information from the British?'

The Nawab looked sad and hurt. 'I hope you don't think I would do that, Olivia.'

'Of course I don't!' she cried immediately. 'How can you think that, Harry?'

On Sunday evenings Douglas and Olivia used to walk in the Satipur graveyard, and read the names of the dead. 'I'm sorry I can't offer you anything more exciting than a walk round a graveyard,' said Douglas sadly. 'Think of your sister Marcia in

The Nawab turned away. 'Olivia, who has told you these stories about the robbers?' he said.

Paris! She can go to the theatre, the cinema, a restaurant – but there's nothing to do here.'

'Don't be silly, darling,' said Olivia softly, and took his arm. 'I don't want to be in Paris, I want to be here with you.'

They had come to a grave they often visited, because Olivia liked what was written on the gravestone:

E.A. Edwards, died in 1857, aged 29. A brave officer, a good son, a kind father, but most of all a dear husband. . .

'Just like you, darling,' she told Douglas. 'Except you're not a kind father yet.'

'But I will be,' he promised.

'Of course you will.'

But in fact she was beginning to get quite worried. Why wasn't she pregnant? Was something wrong? She could not believe it. Surely a young, handsome, healthy couple like herself and Douglas must be able to have children, a lot of beautiful, brave children. He too was sure of it. Perhaps she was not pregnant because she had been frightened by all the little babies in the graveyard, who had died of disease and the terrible Indian heat.

She had brought some flowers for the Saunders' baby. They found the grave, with its expensive Italian statue, and she placed her flowers there. Then she turned to Douglas and whispered happily, 'I made a wish . . . You know, like at Baba Firdaus' shrine on the Husband's Wedding Day, when women ask to have a baby . . .' They both smiled. Then she became serious and said, 'Douglas, what is all this about gangs of robbers?'

'There's a gang, robbing and killing in the villages around Khatm. All the village people are frightened of them.'

'How terrible! But the Nawab isn't involved, is he?'

'That's the point. We think he *is* involved – he protects the robbers and they pay him.'

'That can't be true,' said Olivia. 'He wouldn't do that.'

Douglas laughed at her innocence. They walked on, but she was no longer interested in the graves. 'But he's a prince,' she said, 'He wouldn't get involved with criminals. Anyway, he's a rich man. He wouldn't need the money.' And then suddenly, 'Oh let's go. This place is depressing me.'

'I thought you liked it here,' said Douglas, looking offended.

'I only like the trees.' She turned and walked away from him. She was angry both with him and the dead soldiers in their graves. She stopped again by the Saunders' baby's grave and stayed there for a moment. It was getting darker now, and there were shadows all around her. Her heart was full of sadness. She did not know why; perhaps because she was not having a baby. She thought if only she had a baby – a strong, fair-haired, blue-eyed boy – everything would be all right. She and Douglas would both be happy, and they would agree about everything.

'Come on now,' said Douglas crossly. 'It's getting dark.' She got up, but then suddenly fell to her knees again and covered her face with her hands. The white statue of the angel looked down at her. The last birds stopped singing, and Olivia cried quietly in the silence. Douglas walked slowly back to her, but he too was silent as he waited for her.

'Sorry,' she said after a while, wiping her eyes. She got up, but he did not help her.

'You should have gone to the mountains,' he said stiffly. 'It's too hot for you here. That's why you're so upset.'

'Yes, that's why,' she said. She was glad he believed that.

Diary 15 June

Death of a beggar woman

One of the town's beggars is a very old woman. At least, she looks very old, but perhaps that's because she has been poor all her life. She doesn't ask for money, but when she is hungry, she stands there with her hand stretched out, waiting for food. I never see her talking to anyone. She doesn't seem to have a home, or even a favourite place to sleep. When she is tired she lies down in the street, so that people have to walk round her.

A few days ago, I took some dirty clothes to the man who does our washing. He lives near our house. I think I saw the old beggar woman lying in his street. I'm not sure. The trouble is, I'm so used to her that I hardly notice her. But I did notice her when I went back to fetch the clean clothes. There was something strange about the way she was lying. There is a heap of rubbish in the street, and she was lying almost on top of it, with flies all around her.

The people in the street were not interested when I told them about her. They didn't have time to listen. I wondered if perhaps she was dead. Who would take her away? Nobody was responsible for her, and I certainly wasn't, so I went home carrying my clean clothes.

Later I was angry with myself. I had not even bothered to go close to see if she was alive or dead. I told Inder Lal about her. He was getting ready to leave for his office, but I persuaded him to come with me. We stood at the corner of the street, and I could see she was still there.

'Is she alive?' I asked him.

'I don't know,' he answered, moving away. 'I don't think we should go closer. Anyway it's time for me to go to the office. I mustn't be late.'

I decided I had to see, so I went closer.

'No, don't!' cried Inder Lal. He even rang his bicycle bell to stop me. But I went right up to the old woman. Her eyes were open and she was alive, but she was very ill, and rather dirty. There was a terrible smell, and the flies were all over her.

'Go on, go to your office!' I cried to Inder Lal. I didn't want him to get dirty or catch the old woman's disease. He turned away gladly, in his fresh clean clothes, and cycled off to work. For the first time I understood – really felt – the Hindu fear of dirt and disease. I went home and washed myself again and again. I was afraid. Those flies could easily have given me the old woman's illness.

Later I went to the local hospital, the same one where Dr Saunders used to work in Olivia's time. It is too small for Satipur now, so there are patients sleeping outside on the grass as well as on the floors inside. I met the chief doctor, Dr Gopal, a handsome Indian in a white coat. He was very polite and sympathetic, and said that if I brought the old woman in, they would look after her.

'Could she be collected by ambulance?' I asked.

'Unfortunately, the ambulance is being repaired,' he answered, 'but anyway we only use it in an emergency.'

'But this *is* an emergency,' I said.

The doctor smiled sadly. 'Are you from England?' he asked. Although he was very busy, he seemed to want to talk, perhaps to practise his English. 'We have many patients in this hospital,' he said. 'The patients and some of the nurses can't even read, so sometimes a patient gets the wrong medicine. It's not like in England, you know. If this old woman is dying, there is not much we can do to help.'

'But then where should she die?' I asked.

'You see our problem,' he said. 'This hospital is old, we haven't enough beds or nurses or equipment.' He went on, giving a long list of his difficulties. I could see he liked practising his English, but he was also glad to be able to tell his troubles to someone. 'We cannot avoid making mistakes. It is all very difficult. I'm always trying to find more people to work here, but they are often no good at the job. What can I do?' He spoke English well. His feelings were deep and his life was difficult. He looked at me across the desk with the same eyes as Inder Lal's, wanting my help and understanding.

I understood his problem, but I also understood that he could not help me with the beggar woman. I would have to look after her by myself. Everyone else had too many problems of their own. What could I do? There was no ambulance to bring her to hospital, so I would have to pay for a taxi for her. But I would have to lift her into the taxi myself, because nobody else would want to touch her in case they caught her disease. And could I persuade a taxi driver to take a dirty, dying, old beggar woman?

I left Dr Gopal's office and walked through the hospital, stepping over patients lying on the floor. I was thinking of the question I had asked Dr Gopal: 'Then where should she die?' It had seemed an important question to me at the time, but it no longer seemed like that. What did it really matter, one more death in this country of millions? This was a new idea to me, that the old woman could die, and it wouldn't matter to anybody. I was surprised at myself. I realized I was changing, becoming more like the Indians, who accept birth and death as everyday events. But perhaps, I thought, as I'm living in India, it's better to be like them. Perhaps there isn't even any choice – the country itself is changing me as it has changed other people.

Walking back from the hospital, I passed the place where Maji, the holy woman, lived, and stopped to talk to her. She looked sharply into my face and asked at once, 'What's the matter?'

'It's the old beggar woman. I think she's dying,' I answered.

My voice sounded almost bored, like all the other people that day, but Maji surprised me by jumping up and shouting, 'What! Leelavati? Her time has come?'

Leelavati! The beggar woman had a name! Suddenly the whole problem became urgent again. We hurried off together to the street where I had last seen her. But she had gone, and when we asked the local people, they didn't know where she was.

But Maji said, 'I know where she may be.' We hurried off again, through the market, then out of town to the shrines of the dead widows.

'Ah!' cried Maji. 'There she is! I knew it!' The old woman was lying under a tree. She looked worse than before. Maji went up to her and said, 'I've been looking for you. Why didn't you call me?'

The old woman was staring up into the sky but I don't think she could see anything. Maji sat down and took the old woman's head on to her knees. She moved her hands gently over the old head, and looked down into the dying face. Suddenly the old woman smiled, her toothless mouth open like a baby's. Could she see Maji, looking down at her like a mother? Or did she just *feel* Maji's love for her? That smile seemed like a miracle to me.

I sat with them under the tree. There had been a particularly bad dust storm that day, but now, at the end of the day, the light was very clear. The sky was bright blue and the air was fresh and clean.

'You see,' said Maji, 'I knew she would come here.' She continued to hold the old woman's head. She was smiling and happy, full of love for Leelavati and proud that she, Maji, was helping an old friend to die well. She told me about the beggar woman's life. When her husband died, his family had refused to let her stay in the house, and when her parents died, she had no home or money. She had to beg to stay alive, and travelled from town to town, until she arrived in Satipur ten years ago. Here she fell ill, and could not travel any more, so she had just stayed.

'But now she is tired,' said Maji. 'Now it is time. Now she has loved, and worked, and travelled, and begged, enough.' And again she gently touched the old face, smiling into it.

It was pleasant sitting here, in the cool of the evening, and we were ready to stay for hours. But she did not keep us waiting long. As the light disappeared, and the sky and air turned pale silver, and the birds fell asleep in the dark trees, at that lovely hour she died. I would not have noticed, as she had not moved for a long time. She made no noise or movement. She just stopped breathing. Maji was very pleased. She said Leelavati had done well in life, and that's why she had been given a good, a holy death.

1923
Olivia is still not pregnant

One day Olivia told Douglas that Harry was lying ill at Khatm, and that she wanted to go and visit him. Douglas said 'Oh?' and nothing more. Now at last Douglas knew about her visits to Khatm, at least that was what she wanted to believe. She did not want to lie to him, she wanted to be honest with him and have his permission to visit the Nawab. But at the same time she knew she did not want to give up these visits, and dared not tell her husband the whole truth, in case he ordered her never to go there again.

So now Olivia felt much happier, and never hurried back from Khatm in order to arrive before Douglas. If he came home before she did, she could always tell him quite truthfully that she had been to visit poor sick Harry. But Douglas never came home early. He seemed to have more and more work at the office, and when he came home he was so tired that he went to bed very soon. But Olivia went to bed late, and usually got up late in the morning too.

However, one morning she was awake, and sat with him while he ate a large cooked breakfast. As she watched him chewing the meat, she suddenly realized his face was fatter and his body was heavier than before. It made him look more like the other Englishmen in India. She stopped herself thinking that immediately – what a terrible idea!

'Douglas,' she said, 'Harry is still ill.'

'Oh?' He went on chewing his food slowly.

'Could we ask Dr Saunders to look at him?'

'Dr Saunders doesn't take private patients.'

'But he's the only English doctor round here.' And when

Douglas did not even look up at her, Olivia added, 'And Harry *is* English.'

Douglas had finished eating, and now started to smoke his pipe. He did everything slowly and carefully; that was his way. She had always loved him for his English calmness; he was a quiet, brave, honest man. But now suddenly she thought: what a husband! He can't even make me pregnant!

She cried crossly, 'Must you smoke that pipe? In this heat?'

He stayed calm. 'You should have gone to the mountains,' he said.

'To do what? To go for walks with Mrs Crawford? To go to the same boring old dinner parties? If I go to one more of those, I'll die!' She held her head in her hands.

Douglas went on smoking. It was very quiet in the room. The servants took away the dirty plates as quietly as possible, because they did not want to stop the argument. After a while Olivia said, 'I'm sorry, Douglas. I don't know what's the matter with me.'

'I told you. It's the heat. It's too much for an Englishwoman.'

'You're probably right,' she replied quietly. 'In fact, I'd like to see Dr Saunders myself.'

He looked at her with his clear honest eyes.

'Because,' she explained shyly, 'I'm not getting pregnant.'

He left his pipe on the table, and went into their bedroom, where there were no servants to listen. She followed him. They held each other, and she whispered, 'I don't want anything to change . . . I don't want *you* to change.'

'I'm not changing,' he said.

'No, you're not,' she agreed. But she held him even more closely. She wanted so much to be pregnant. Everything would be all right then – he would not change, she would not change, they would be a family as they had planned.

'You should have gone to the mountains,' Douglas said. 'The heat is too much for an Englishwoman.'

'Wait a while,' he said. 'It'll be all right. You'll get pregnant.'

'You think so?'

'I'm sure.'

She held on to his strong arm and went out with him to the front of the house. Although it was so early, the air was heavy and hot.

'It's so bad for you here,' he said. 'This awful heat.'

'But I feel fine!' She laughed – because she really did.

'If I can get a holiday, we could both go to the mountains.'

'You think you can? Oh, you don't have to for me. I'm fine,' she said again.

Douglas looked down at her lovely face. That morning it was difficult for him to leave. 'I'll talk to Dr Saunders about Harry,' he said.

As he rode away, Olivia waved to him until she could no longer see him. Then she turned and looked the other way, towards Khatm, towards the Palace. There was nothing to be seen, as the same dust covered everything. But it was true what she had told Douglas: she felt fine, the heat and dust did not bother her. Something inside her kept her cheerful and happy.

Later that morning she decided to see Dr Saunders. There was still time before the Nawab's car came to collect her. But when she walked to the Saunders' house, the doctor had already left and only his wife was at home. Olivia was surprised to find that Mrs Saunders was not in bed, but was sitting in one of the big empty rooms, looking miserable.

'I'm still ill,' she told Olivia. 'I should be in bed. I want to be in bed. But the servants . . . we white women have to be very careful, you know. If they see me in bed all the time, they might get the wrong idea . . .'

'Might they?' said Olivia, not quite understanding.

'Oh yes,' said Mrs Saunders confidently. 'You hear a lot of stories when you've been in India for a few years. There was a lady in Northern India . . . Her husband was away, and suddenly one night her servant rushed into her bedroom and . . . well, it was all very shocking.' She looked round to make sure no servants were listening, and whispered, 'These Indians get excited very easily. Some people say it's their hot food. I don't know about that, but I'm sure of one thing, Mrs Rivers, they've got just one idea in their heads, and that's to "you-know-what" with a white woman.'

Olivia stared at Mrs Saunders' thin face. Could she really be so afraid of Indians? She seemed so sure, so confident that there was danger. No, Olivia could not believe it. The idea was nonsense! She jumped up. It was time to go – the Nawab's car would be at her house now.

*

When Olivia suggested to the Nawab that they should send for Dr Saunders, the Nawab laughed. He said that if a European doctor was needed he would send for one from England or Germany if necessary. But to keep Olivia and Harry happy he sent a car to collect Dr Saunders.

The doctor was pleased to be sent for by an Indian prince, and spoke for a long time about Harry's illness, using all the long medical words he could think of. The Nawab was so polite to him that Olivia realized it was his way of laughing at the doctor. Harry and Olivia both found the situation very funny and could not hide their laughter. The Nawab was delighted his guests were enjoying themselves, and invited Dr Saunders to lunch.

As the doctor ate and drank, he talked more and more. Encouraged by the Nawab, he gave his opinion of Indians and told stories about his life in India.

'Then, you see, Nawab Sahib, I called the man to my office and hit him.'

'Very good, doctor,' said the Nawab, enthusiastically. 'Quite right.'

'It's the only way to manage them, Nawab Sahib. You can't argue with them. They're not as intelligent as we are, you know.'

'Exactly, doctor. How well you understand them!'

Dr Saunders seemed to forget that the Nawab was Indian himself. It was amusing for a while, but soon Olivia and Harry stopped enjoying it. The Nawab noticed immediately, and in the middle of the meal, left the table, calling Harry and Olivia to follow him. All three of them ran up to Harry's room, where the Nawab threw himself into an armchair and laughed long and loudly. He was surprised when the other two did not laugh.

'I invited him and made him talk, just to amuse you two!' he complained. 'Why don't you laugh? He's very funny.'

'He's so stupid,' said Olivia. 'I almost feel sorry for him. He doesn't make me laugh.' And Harry agreed.

'But he thinks we Indians are stupid!' cried the Nawab.

'Don't think about him,' said Harry. 'He's just boring. Why did you bring him here?'

'*She* wanted him,' and the Nawab pointed accusingly at Olivia. But when she looked upset, he said, 'Anyway, I don't think he's boring, I think he's very funny.' Then suddenly his mood changed. 'You are right,' he said crossly. 'He isn't amusing at all. Let's send him away.'

Olivia felt she had to say, 'He really is awful. Don't judge by him.'

The Nawab looked at her rather coldly. 'Don't judge what by him?' he asked.

'All of us,' she replied.

'Who do you mean by *us*?' asked Harry. He too sounded cold, almost angry. Olivia felt confused. It was the same feeling she had experienced at the Crawfords' dinner party. She did not understand the situation.

'I don't know how *you* feel,' added Harry, 'but I don't want to be part of a group that includes the Crawfords and the Minnies —'

'But Harry,' she cried, 'they're not as bad as Dr Saunders! And then there's Douglas and —'

'You?' said Harry.

'All are the same,' said the Nawab suddenly and heavily.

Olivia had a shock – did he mean her too? She was frightened by the feelings she saw so clearly in his angry handsome face. She desperately wished not to be included in the group of people who made him angry. She felt she would do anything to be one of the people he liked.

'I shall send him away,' said the Nawab, calling loudly for servants. 'Put Dr Saunders in a car and send him home,' he told them. 'Oh, and pay him. *You* do it. Just give him the money, he'll take it,' and both the Nawab and his servant laughed. They knew how offended Dr Saunders would be to receive money from a servant.

Olivia was almost crying. Perhaps he wanted her to go as well. 'I'd better go too,' she said, her voice trembling.

'You?' said the Nawab. 'With *him*? Do you think I would let you go home in the same car as him? Is that what you think of my friendship?' He sounded very upset.

'But I have to go home soon – and as the car is going to Satipur...' she protested. But now she was laughing, and suddenly felt terribly light-hearted.

'Another car will go. Ten cars will go if necessary. Sit down please. Oh, this is silly, we are all unhappy when we should be enjoying ourselves. Harry! Olivia! Please be cheerful!' and he called his young men to sing and dance for them. For the rest of that day Olivia had a very pleasant time.

Diary 20 June

Inder Lal and I visit the shrine

Here in Satipur the weather is the same every year. It gets hotter and hotter, until at last the rain comes. People say that the hotter it is, the more rain there will be. So we want it to be hot. And by now we have all accepted the heat, not got used to it, but accepted it. And we are all too tired to complain much. The heat brings some advantages too. In a really hot summer the fruit tastes sweeter and the flowers are more colourful. At night, plants and flowers have a wonderful smell, and there are delicious iced drinks you can buy in the market.

On Sunday Inder Lal and I went to Baba Firdaus' shrine for a picnic. His wife was still away on her pilgrimage. We got very hot on the bus journey and then climbing the steep path, but when we arrived at the shrine, it seemed like heaven. The sun could not get through the leaves of the trees, and the stream was cool and fresh. Inder Lal lay down at once to sleep under a tree, but I was so delighted with the place that I wandered around it. Last time I had been there, on the Husband's Wedding Day, there had been hundreds of people laughing and shouting. Now there was only the sound of the water and the birds.

When Inder Lal woke up, we ate the sandwiches I had brought for us. He had never had sandwiches before and ate them with interest, always glad to have a new experience.

'Something else that is new to me,' he said, 'is going on an excursion with only one other person. In India we usually go out in a crowd of family and friends. I think it's more interesting to have a conversation between only two people. Then they can tell each other the secrets they keep in their hearts.'

I waited for him to tell me his secrets, but he only asked, 'Do you often go on picnics in England?' and 'Do you always eat sandwiches?'

'Yes,' I answered. He went on eagerly asking me questions.

'Do you like the countryside? This is for my information only, you know.' He often says this when asking questions. He loves collecting useless facts. His mother does the same with things. She picks up paper, empty bottles, pieces of cloth, and keeps them in case they can be used in the future.

'Look what I have brought,' he said. He showed me two pieces of red string. He said we had to tie them to the shrine and wish. He tied his piece first, shut his eyes and wished.

'I thought it was only for women who want babies,' I said.

'All wishes are heard,' he said. 'Now you do it.' He watched me with great interest. 'You can say your wish aloud, if you are alone or have only one friend with you.'

I smiled but didn't tell him my wish. We went back to sit under the tree. He was really eager to know.

'Tell me,' he begged.

'Well, what do you think?' I asked him.

'How can I say? I can't know what you are thinking. But if you tell me your wish,' he said cleverly, 'I will tell you mine.'

'Let's try and guess,' I suggested.

'You first.' He enjoyed this game.

I pretended to be thinking hard. 'I think,' I said in the end, 'your wish had something to do with your office.'

At once he looked surprised and upset. 'How did you know?'

'Oh, I just guessed.'

Now he became depressed, and no longer enjoyed the game. He was thinking of his problems at work, and wasn't interested in my wish any more.

But now I wanted him to be. I really wanted, as he had said, to tell someone my secrets, although it is difficult enough to tell a friend who knows about my life and problems. How much more difficult it was to tell him, who didn't know me at all! The trouble was, when I tied my string, there was nothing I really wanted to wish for. It's not that I have everything, but there are so many things I haven't got that I need more than one wish. So I didn't have a secret to tell him.

But at that moment there was one thing I wanted very much: to get close to him. And as it seemed impossible to explain this in words, I put my hand on his. Then he looked at me in quite a different way. I could feel his hand tremble under mine. He looked almost afraid; he did not know what to do next, or what I was going to do next. I could see how all those stories about European women rushed through his head. But there we were, a healthy young Indian, whose wife was away, and a European girl, in a beautiful, lonely place. It was getting dark. We made love under the tree.

Afterwards he said, 'This is the secret of the Husband's Wedding Day. This is how that Hindu woman in the old story became pregnant, you know, not a miracle at all!' and he laughed for a long time at his joke.

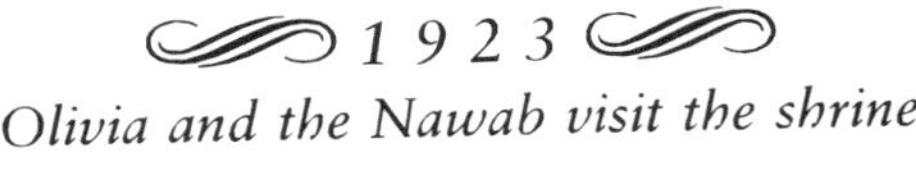

1923

Olivia and the Nawab visit the shrine

One day the Nawab's car arrived to fetch Olivia, but this time Harry was in it. She wanted to leave at once, but he wanted to rest in her cool sitting room for a while. He went on sitting there.

She became impatient. 'Let's go, Harry. If we don't leave soon, it'll get too hot.'

'No, play something for me,' he said. 'I haven't heard you play the piano for a long time.'

'And then we'll go,' she said.

For a few minutes she played and Harry listened, but suddenly she stopped and banged the piano lid. 'I haven't practised lately. And it's too hot to play. And just listen to the piano, it's in terrible condition. Come on, Harry, let's go.'

'You could send for the man from Bombay, to repair it.'

'Oh, I don't often play now.'

'What a pity.' He said it so deliberately that she began to think about it. Why hadn't she been playing lately? There must be a reason, but she couldn't think of it.

'It's so nice here, Olivia,' said Harry. 'I don't feel I ever want to leave. I feel like a man in the desert who has just found water.'

'Don't be silly, Harry. Khatm isn't a desert.'

'How tough you are, Olivia. You don't mind anything, the heat, the dust, anything! And you're never ill, are you?'

'Of course not. Why should I be ill? People often *think* they're ill. But I don't.'

'Last night I was so ill again. And I haven't eaten Indian food for weeks. I don't understand it.'

'I told you. Some people imagine they're ill. I think you're like that.'

'You may be right.' He shut his eyes in pain. 'You know, I feel I can't live in India another day.'

She tried to be sympathetic but she was so impatient to leave! They could hear the sound of a drum from the servants' part of the house.

'I can feel it beating in my head,' said Harry, his eyes still closed.

'That? Oh, I don't notice that any more. They're always beating the drum, for a wedding, or a death or something. Harry, we must go, or it'll be too hot in the car.'

Harry said slowly and carefully, 'I don't want to go.'

Olivia could not believe it. She tried to control her voice but it trembled as she spoke.

'What about the car?' she asked.

'We'll send it back.'

Olivia said nothing, but stared at the floor. Harry looked carefully at her, then said very gently, 'What's the matter with you, Olivia? Why are you so eager to go?'

'Because we've been invited.' That sounded silly, so she became cross with him. 'Anyway, you don't think I *like* sitting round here all day waiting for Douglas to come home, do you? I'd go mad if I stayed here alone all day. I have to go out.'

'Is that why you like coming to the Palace?'

She did not answer him directly. 'Douglas knows I go to the Palace. He knew I'd been to see you when you were ill.'

'Yes, to see *me*,' said Harry accusingly.

'Harry, you're jealous! That's what it is. You want to be the only one – the only guest in the Palace, I mean.' Her face was red as she corrected herself.

'All right,' he said. 'We'll go.'

He went to the door, putting on his sun hat. She felt she should not hurry after him. She wanted to show him she did not mind much about going. But then she discovered that she did mind, very much, so she followed him quickly to the car.

The journey was unpleasant, and not only because of the heat and dust. Neither of them spoke. Suddenly Harry said, 'There he is!'

The Nawab had come to meet them in another car. 'Where have you been?' he said. 'I've been waiting and waiting. I've come to meet you because I want to go to Baba Firdaus' shrine.'

'I'm sorry, I don't feel like going there,' Harry said. 'I just want to go home.'

The Nawab turned at once to Olivia. 'You come, Olivia,' he said.

'All right,' she answered, and got into his car beside him. As they drove away, they saw the other car drive back to the Palace, with Harry in the back seat looking cross.

'Why does he look like that?' the Nawab asked Olivia. 'Do you

The Nawab turned at once to Olivia. 'You come, Olivia,' he said.

think he is ill?' He seemed very worried about Harry and went on talking about him. 'I know he is often unhappy and wants to go home to England. And I want him to go too, but at the same time – Olivia, can you understand this, does it sound very selfish? – I don't want to lose him. I see you do think I am selfish,' he ended sadly.

She knew she did not need to contradict him. She was there to listen, and she was happy to do that. It was also good to be next to him and to look occasionally at his handsome face, as he concentrated on the road.

'Often I have wanted to say to him, Harry, your mother wants you at home, go. Sometimes I *have* said it. Once his bag was packed and he even had his ticket. At the last moment I broke down – I could not let him go. And he said, "No, I want to stay" . . . Now we must walk, Olivia. Will it be too hot for you?'

They climbed together up the steep path to the shrine. She was listening to him talking, so she hardly noticed the sun beating down. It was extremely hot.

'Life becomes very hard if particular people are absent. Once I asked a very holy man why *these* people are important. He answered, and I like his answer very much, that these are the people who once sat close to you in heaven. It is a beautiful idea, isn't it, Olivia? That we once sat close together in heaven.'

But just as they arrived at the trees and the stream, some violent-looking men came out of the shrine. Olivia had a shock. They had hard faces and guns, and for a moment they stared dangerously at Olivia and the Nawab. But as soon as they recognized the Nawab, they fell at his feet and greeted him.

He asked Olivia to sit under a tree and wait. She watched him talk to the men. They looked like dangerous criminals, but their faces showed their love for the Nawab. He sent them away quite soon, then took her into the shrine.

'Look what I've brought,' he said, holding out two pieces of red string. She tied hers to the shrine, then he tied his.

'What did you wish?' he asked.

'Perhaps I shouldn't tell,' she replied, smiling at him.

'You can if there is only one person here with you. You know what women come here for? What they wish for? Is that what you wished for too?'

'Yes,' she said.

'Ah.'

After a silence he said, 'You have heard the story of the Husband's Wedding Day? Just a story of course. I suppose it may be true – there are many stories of miracles that have happened. But I think modern people like you and I shouldn't believe it . . .'

'Who were those men?' asked Olivia suddenly. There was a pause.

'Who do you think they were?' He looked sharply at her, then laughed. 'I suppose you think they are bad men. Perhaps you believe the stories people tell about me. But I don't think they are bad men, because they came to a holy place, this shrine, to bring flowers and thank God.' He pointed to the fresh flowers lying outside the shrine, and looked closely at her face. Perhaps he was wondering if she believed him. But she was not thinking about that at all. In fact she did not really hear his words. She felt his presence, his closeness to her, and her whole body was alive and aware of him. Now he concentrated all his attention on her alone.

'Come,' he said. 'Sit with me.' They sat just outside the shrine. In the distance Olivia could see the heat in the air, but here under the trees it was pleasantly cool.

'When we leave here, Olivia, will you go back to Satipur and tell them yes, the Nawab is bad, now I have seen with my own eyes that he meets robbers and criminals secretly. Will you go back and say that, Olivia?'

This time she did not hesitate to answer. 'Do you really believe I'd do that?' she said, so honestly that he accepted her answer immediately. He touched her arm with his fingers.

'No, I don't believe you would,' he said. 'And that is why I open my heart to you and tell you everything. Please don't think I want you to say only that the Nawab is a good person. Of course I would like to be a good person – we are all trying to be that – but I am very far from that. Very far,' he added, looking sad.

'Who isn't?' said Olivia sympathetically. He touched her arm again. Partly she wished he wouldn't, but partly she wanted him to do it again.

'You are right. We are all far from good. But there are some people,' he said, pausing to let her think who they were, 'who judge other people, and who think they know everything. Major Minnies, for example. How dare he tell *me* what to do? Me! The Nawab Sahib of Khatm!' For a moment he could not speak. 'Do you know how my family became Nawabs, Olivia? It was in 1817. Amanullah Khan had been fighting for many years. Sometimes he fought other Indian princes, sometimes he fought the British. He had a very exciting life, Olivia! I would like to live like that. Even the British were afraid of him. When they saw they could not win against him, they offered him the region of Khatm and asked him to be the Nawab. They were clever people! Because he was tired of fighting, he accepted.' He looked at Olivia with sad eyes. 'But you can get tired also sitting in a palace. Then you feel it would be better to fight your enemies and kill them. Don't you think it is better to meet your enemies openly, Olivia? Better than making secret plans.' He seemed suddenly very upset.

She put out her hand and touched his chest. He said, 'How kind you are to me.' He put his hand on hers, and held it to his heart. She felt very close to him, closer than she had ever felt to anybody before. She could not escape him now, even if she had wanted to.

'Not here,' he said. He led her away from the shrine, and they made love under a tree. Afterwards he made a joke. 'This is the secret of the Husband's Wedding Day. This is why the woman became pregnant. It wasn't a miracle at all!'

'Then why did you make me tie the string? It wasn't necessary!' Olivia said.

He laughed and laughed, delighted with her.

Diary 31 July

Am I pregnant?

Maji tells me I am pregnant. At first I didn't believe her, it's too early to know. But she was so sure that I have begun to believe her. I think she knows things that most people don't.

One day she told me that she used to be a midwife. I was very surprised at this, but she laughed and explained. She had been married and had children, but her husband had not worked much, so she had to earn money. Her mother and grandmother had both been midwives and had taught her everything they knew, so it became her job too. But after her husband's death she went on pilgrimages all over India, and in the end came to Satipur and decided to stay. She doesn't need to work now, as her friends bring her food.

I was so interested in her life story that I forgot about myself. But she put her hand on my stomach and asked, 'What are you going to do? I can help you if you want help. Do you understand what I mean?' I realized she was offering me an abortion.

'You will be safe with me,' she added. 'I haven't worked as a midwife for years but I have helped many women in the past.' She went on to tell me stories of pregnant women and abortions she had carried out. I didn't give her an answer at the time, but on my way home in the rain, I thought about her offer.

Diary 15 August

Chid, Inder Lal and I

Chid has come back from his pilgrimage. He looks so different that at first I didn't recognize him. He no longer wears his orange robe, but he has found some shorts, a shirt and shoes. His hair is growing again too. He doesn't look like a Hindu holy man any more. He is also very quiet, and he is ill again.

He sleeps a lot in the corner of my room. He hasn't explained why he left Inder Lal's mother and Ritu on the pilgrimage, nor why he has changed so much. He just says, 'I hate the smell' (Well, of course, I know what he means – Indians live and eat differently from us and do have a different smell) and 'I hate the food.' He only eats plain boiled food now, and likes English soup best.

Inder Lal is not pleased about Chid's return. He can see that Chid isn't a holy person any more. I should also explain that, since our picnic at the shrine, Inder Lal has started sleeping in my room at night. I'm sure the neighbours have noticed, but they don't mind. They realize he is lonely, while his wife is away.

So when Chid came back, Inder Lal at first felt shy about visiting me at night. But I have explained to him that Chid just sleeps, and doesn't notice us at all. Inder Lal and I lie on my sleeping bag together, and talk, and make love. He is a very kind, loving person. It is more and more delightful to be with him.

I haven't told him about my pregnancy yet, although I tried to. I met him after work and took him to the old British graveyard. He liked the Italian statue over the Saunders' baby's grave. I showed him the British officer's grave (the one Olivia liked) and read out what it said:

A good son, a kind father, but most of all a dear husband . . .

'Like you,' I told him.

'I have no choice,' he said, looking depressed.

He doesn't seem to enjoy having a family. So I have decided not to tell him about my pregnancy. I don't want to destroy the happiness we share at the moment.

1923
Olivia tells the Nawab and Douglas about her pregnancy

When Olivia discovered she was pregnant, she did not tell Douglas. She put it off from day to day. In the end, she told the Nawab first.

One morning as she arrived at the Palace, she found all the servants packing for a journey.

'We're going to the hills at last!' Harry told her. 'The Begum has decided.'

'Oh?' said Olivia. Although she was never invited to see the Begum, she knew that Harry played cards with her every day.

'But there's another reason,' added Harry. 'Major Minnies is angry with the Nawab. He's talking to him now.'

'Why? You must tell me, Harry. I need to . . . I mean, I want to know. Why is he angry?'

'Well, the Nawab's in trouble. You know he has very little money left. And the British are always ordering him to do things. I hate it when Major Minnies comes here. The Nawab is always so upset after that. He's terribly sensitive, Olivia, and the British threaten him —'

'How dare they!' cried Olivia.

'You see, he's not an important prince, so the British can threaten him. But he feels so offended . . .'

They heard his voice outside. He rushed in, very angry.

'I cannot talk to Major Minnies. It's like talking to a servant. You can tell him that next time, Harry. Or perhaps you would not like to say that to him.' He looked fiercely at Harry and Olivia. 'But you are both the same. I don't know why you stay with me. You want to be with other English people. You feel nothing for me at all!'

'We're going to the hills at last! The Begum has decided.'

'You know that's not true,' said Harry quietly.

The Nawab went out and Olivia followed him. She called his name, which she had never used before, and he turned in surprise and waited for her. She ran to meet him, and told him in a whisper, there on the stairs, that she was pregnant.

After that she felt she had to tell Douglas too, so she told him that same night.

The next day was very long. She waited all day, not for Douglas, but for a message from the Palace. Had they left for the hills? Surely they would have told her. She decided that if they had left, she would tell Douglas she must escape from the heat and go to the mountains immediately. She could not stay.

When Douglas and Major Minnies arrived for dinner, they told her about the Nawab's gang of robbers who had robbed and hurt some village people near Satipur. The Major had been turned away from the Palace when he went to complain to the Nawab.

'But they're in the hills!' said Olivia. 'Harry told me,' she added carefully.

'They didn't go because at the last moment the Begum decided she didn't want to,' said the Major.

Olivia laughed. She suddenly felt very cheerful – they had not left!

'I hope this time the government will punish the Nawab,' said Douglas angrily. 'It's time to teach him a lesson.'

'He's not a schoolboy!' cried Olivia.

'In some ways,' the Major said to Olivia, 'he's a fine man, but he hasn't much self-control. I still like him. And I think you do too.'

'Yes,' she said.

'He's the worst kind of Indian, and he's the worst kind of prince you could have,' said Douglas.

'Perhaps you're right,' said the Major. After thinking for a moment he said slowly, 'Sometimes I think I'm not the right kind of person to be in India. Of course I would never change my job. But I do see the other side of the argument too easily. I get too close to the Indians. The Nawab, for example. He interests me very, very much. He interests you too, doesn't he?' he asked Olivia.

'Does he, darling?' laughed Douglas.

'Well,' said Olivia, laughing back, 'he *is* very interesting. And terribly handsome.'

'Really?' said Douglas, who had never noticed.

'He loves adventure,' said the Major. 'He gets bored in his palace. That's when he starts talking about Amanullah Khan and *his* exciting life. I used to know the Nawab's father, you know. He went to Europe and brought back a dancer who lived at the Palace for years. In fact she had Harry's room, and that's where the old Nawab died, with her. He loved Indian poems too, let me see, I can remember some that he wrote . . .'

And as the Major spoke the beautiful words of the old Nawab's poem, Douglas took his wife's hand in the dark. 'Happy, darling?' he whispered. She smiled at him and he kissed her hand. Then she laughed to herself. So Major Minnies thought that he was too interested in Indians, that he got too close to them! What did *he* know about it? A few Indian poems on a moonlit night. . . ? She laughed out loud at this, and Douglas, who thought she laughed because she was happy, was very happy too.

Next time Olivia saw Harry she asked him, 'Did you know the old Nawab died in this room? With an English dancer?'

Harry started laughing and told her the whole story. After the old Nawab's death, the Begum had ordered the girl to give back any jewels he had given her, before she left the Palace. At first she refused, but the Begum was cleverer than she was. One day the girl escaped from the Palace and arrived in Satipur, dressed in night clothes and asking desperately for help. She was terribly upset, and accused the Begum of trying to poison her. The British officials arranged to send her home on the next ship. When the Begum offered to send her clothes, the girl refused to touch them. She said there was an old woman at the Palace who could put poison on clothes, so that the person who wore them would die a terribly painful death. 'Oh, you don't know what goes on at the Palace!' the girl had cried.

'She must have been mad!' smiled Olivia. 'Those poor old ladies at the Palace can't hurt anyone.'

These days she was happier with the Nawab than she had ever been. He sent for her every day, and their love was no secret at the Palace. Sometimes he even took her into his own bedroom, where she had not been before. She did anything he wanted. She remembered Harry once saying, 'You don't say no to a person like him.' It was true.

The Nawab was delighted with Olivia's pregnancy. He often touched her stomach gently, and asked, 'Really, you will do this for me? You are not afraid? Oh, how brave you are!' He never doubted the baby was his. He wanted her to stay later and later with him every day, but she had to go back to Douglas.

Once he said, 'No. Stay with me. Stay always. It has to be, very soon now. You have to be here with me.' She knew he did not even consider Douglas; for the Nawab, Douglas simply did not exist.

One Sunday Douglas and Olivia were walking arm in arm in the English graveyard. The sun was hot but the leaves of the trees were clean and wet after the rain. Together they read the words on the British officer's gravestone:

A good son, a kind father, but most of all a dear husband . . .

Douglas turned to kiss Olivia and whispered, 'Do you want our son to be a soldier or an official?'

'How do you know it will be a boy?'

'Oh, I'm sure.' Gently, he touched her stomach. 'You're not afraid? You'll really do this for me? How brave you are.'

The same words the Nawab had used! Olivia turned away, too upset to answer. Douglas supposed she was thinking about the Saunders' baby, and hurried her out of the graveyard.

Diary 20 August

My family history

Douglas wanted a son, and he did have one, not by Olivia, but by his second wife, Tessie. This son (my father) was born in India and came to school in England when he was twelve. In 1947 when India became independent and no longer wanted British officials, Douglas and Tessie came back to England, so my father never visited India again. The Crawfords stayed in India, but after some years they no longer felt happy there, and came home to England. When Tessie and Beth, the two sisters, were both widows, they lived together, and shared their memories of India.

I tried to tell Chid some of this, but it doesn't interest him. He is now very eager to leave India, but he's still ill.

Diary 27 August

Chid wants to leave

Chid is now in hospital. Dr Gopal is looking after him. But I have to go every day to take him food. The hospital workers serve food from a bucket, which only the very poor eat. All the beds are full. When someone dies, another patient takes the bed at once.

But Chid does not notice what is happening around him. He lies in bed with his eyes closed. Sometimes he cries silently. I have already written to his family to ask for a ticket home. Meanwhile he wants to know nothing and see nothing – just to lie there and wait.

Why does he hate India now? And why is he ill? Dr Gopal tried to explain. 'You see, this climate is bad for you people. It's bad for us too. Indians have many diseases, because of the heat, the bad water, the food. Perhaps God didn't really want people to live in a country like India! But where else can we live? You remember, you British used to have your clubs, for British only? Well, now we Indians have our illnesses, for Indians only!' And he threw himself back in his chair to laugh.

Perhaps the doctor is right. Life in India is hard for a European body. But what about the Indian spirit? Some British people have accepted the Indian way of life and continue to live here, like the woman missionary I met on my first night, in Bombay. Yes, and what about Olivia? She decided to stay.

I suppose that when Olivia first came to India she was a very ordinary young woman, pretty and a little selfish. But India must have changed her; India made her leave her husband and live with the Nawab, and stay with him. But I don't know anything about her later life, and I'm more and more curious about it. The only way to find out is to do the same as she did – to stay on.

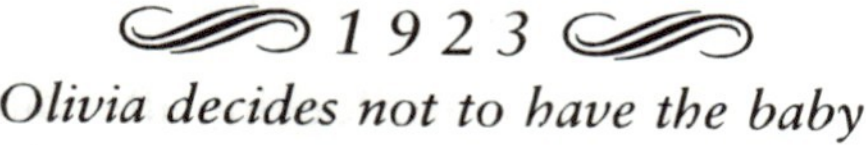

1923

Olivia decides not to have the baby

Harry and Olivia sat in Harry's room at the Palace, looking at the grey cloudy sky outside.

'I told him I wanted to go home,' Harry said. 'I told him I *had* to. He agreed. He said he'd arrange the tickets and everything.'

'I'm glad,' said Olivia. 'Where is he?'

'He's seeing his lawyers. The government is threatening him again. They'll find out it's stupid to make him angry. Do you know what he said last night? He said, "Wait till my son is born! Then the British will look silly!" '

'He said that?' She turned quickly and stared at Harry.

'Well, yes. He said, "When this baby is born, Douglas and all the British are going to have the shock of their lives." '

'Did he mean – the colour? How can he be so sure the baby is his?' Olivia turned back to the window. A soft rain was falling. Everything outside, the garden, the walls, the Palace, everything was grey and wet. 'I've been thinking about having an abortion,' she said.

'Are you mad?' asked Harry.

'I must! You see, Douglas is terribly happy too. He says all Rivers babies have very fair hair and blue eyes. But Harry, Indian babies are born with a lot of black hair. I've seen them. You must help me. Ask your friend the Begum. She'll know a woman who can carry out an abortion.' When he stood, silent, she laughed rather desperately. 'It's easier than putting poison on clothes anyway.'

Diary 31 August

I decide to have the baby

Today I went to see Maji.

'This would be a good time,' she said, 'now you are eight or nine weeks pregnant. Would you like me to help you?'

I said yes, just because I was curious. She made me lie down in her little house, and rubbed my stomach with her strong hands. They were very hot, and it was quite pleasant, but suddenly I cried 'No, please stop!' She stopped at once and we went outside into the bright daylight. The rain had made everything shining green and wet.

It was quite clear to me now that I didn't want an abortion, that I wanted to have my baby. I felt really happy and it was because I was pregnant. In a strange way Maji had helped me to understand that.

1923
Olivia leaves Douglas

One of the Begum's servants took Olivia, dressed in a long robe which even covered her face, to a dirty little house in the back streets of Khatm. There two midwives calmly began their work. The Begum came to watch, and looked closely at Olivia's face as she cried out in pain.

The two midwives had done their work well, and that night Olivia woke Douglas, who took her to the hospital. Olivia lost the baby, and a lot of blood. But Dr Saunders recognized the signs of the Indian midwives' work, and accused Olivia of having an abortion.

So very soon all the British officials heard about it. They were deeply shocked. They all thought that the Nawab had used Olivia as a way of getting his revenge on the British. Even Major Minnies, who was so sympathetic to India and Indians, was sure of it. Douglas did not tell anybody what he thought.

Olivia never returned to Douglas, but escaped from the hospital and went straight to the Palace. Harry said she travelled the fifteen miles from Satipur (she usually did the journey in one of the Nawab's comfortable cars) by public bus. She arrived in a long Indian robe, white-faced and weak.

Harry left India soon after that, and lived a quiet life with his mother in London. Later, after his mother's death, a friend called Ferdie came to live with him. It wasn't until 1938 that he saw the Nawab again, in London.

Olivia never came back to England. The Nawab bought her a house in the mountains, where he visited her occasionally. She stayed there for another thirty-six years, until her death.

Diary

The end of the story, for Olivia and me

In India you are always aware of the mountains, even when they are hidden by rainclouds and mist. Since I've been in India, I've always wanted to come up into the mountains. Now I have managed to climb up to this small town, and just above it, on the steepest side of the mountain, there are several houses, where other Europeans as well as Olivia used to live. They are all dead now, and buried in the old British graveyard. Olivia did not want to be buried; her body was burnt, as she wished. The Nawab had died six years before her, so she must have died alone.

Her house is still there. It is very difficult to reach, especially in heavy rain, so I had to wait a few days before I could climb to it. It stands alone, with a wonderful view. Nobody lives there now. Inside is her piano, her yellow silk cushions and sofas. She must have sat at the window, sewing and occasionally looking out at the view. Outside there is a chair which was used to carry the Nawab up and down the mountain. He had got too fat and lazy to climb.

When the Nawab visited Harry in London, fifteen years had passed since they had last met. The Nawab was fifty, and had become very fat. He had many problems. The British had carried out their threats and appointed officials to control Khatm instead of him, so he no longer felt happy there. He also seemed quite poor. He had to pay for houses for the Begum and her ladies, now

Since I've been in India, I've always wanted to come up into the mountains.

in Bombay, for his wife Sandy, now in Switzerland having treatment for mental illness, and for Olivia in the mountains. In fact he had come to London to ask the British to allow him more money. He didn't bring Olivia, perhaps because he couldn't afford it, perhaps because she didn't want to come.

Harry found it difficult to remember the great love he had felt for the Nawab all those years ago. The Nawab stayed in Harry's and Ferdie's small flat, and life wasn't easy for them while he was there. He broke chairs just by sitting on them, needed huge Indian meals, and was always complaining about the way the British had behaved towards him.

'Don't get so angry,' Harry often said to him. 'You might have a heart attack and die!' When Harry said this, the Nawab always laughed. He never thought about death. In fact this didn't happen for another fifteen years, and in the end he died in the arms of the ancient Begum, not with Olivia.

After Olivia moved to the house the Nawab had bought her, we have no more information about her. The Nawab never spoke about her, or about the way she lived up there in the mountains. Perhaps he never thought about it, but just imagined she was all right with all the comfort and luxury he provided. He visited her, but did not live there. She herself still wrote to her sister Marcia, but her letters were short and uninteresting. She never wrote after the Nawab's death, in 1953, although she lived for six more years.

What was she like? How did she live? Was she lonely? Was she still in love with the Nawab? Looking round her house on the mountainside, I think she lived in almost the same way as in Satipur, and even as in London. She had her elegant sitting room, and her music. I still cannot imagine what she thought about for all those years, or what she was like when she was old. It was raining when I visited her house, so I couldn't see her view from

What did Olivia think about in the mountains – for thirty-six years?

the sitting room window. It might help me to understand, if I could see what she looked at all those years.

I'm renting a room in the town, just as I did in Satipur. We are on the side of the mountain, and I keep looking up, but I can't see anything because of the rain. I want the rain to stop, I want to go on, to climb higher up, I want to see the mountains. I imagine the highest mountains in the world, with the whitest snow and the bluest sky. Perhaps that's also what Olivia saw; perhaps that's the view she had all those years, and that made her stay in India.

I think it will be a long time before I go down to the valley again. First, of course, I'm going to have my baby. There is a religious group who live higher up; their holy men come down to the town to buy food. They spend their time studying religion and ancient writings, and may let me join them. It will be cold and not very comfortable, but it's what I want. I don't know yet how long I shall stay, but it will have to be for some time because as I get larger and heavier, it will be more difficult to climb down again. Anyway, perhaps I shall stay in the mountains, perhaps, like Olivia, for the rest of my life.

GLOSSARY

abortion an operation to stop pregnancy and get rid of a baby
angel a spirit or messenger from God
Begum, the the title of an important Indian lady or princess, often a widow
chief *(adj)* the most important
Christian *(adj)* belonging to the religion based on the life and work of Jesus Christ
cushion a bag made of cloth, filled with something soft, used to sit or lie on
darling a word we say to a person we love
elegant attractive (clothes), attractively arranged (rooms)
evil *(adj)* very bad
fountain a jet or spray of water, which rises and falls, in a park or garden
get used to to learn to accept or adapt to something new
graveyard a place where Christians are buried
guru a religious teacher in India
heat hot weather, or being hot
heaven the place where Christians believe God is
Hindi an Indian language
Hindu *(adj, n)* belonging to, or a person who believes in, Hinduism, the main Indian religion
holy of God, religious
humour (**sense of humour**) being able to see what is amusing in a situation
landlord a man who owns a building, flat or rooms, where other people pay to live
light-hearted happy, unworried

Major the title of a British army officer
make love to have sex
meditate to think deeply, as a religious act
mental of the mind
midwife a woman who is trained to help during a baby's birth
miracle a wonderful event, something unexpected or unexplained
missionary a person who is sent abroad to do religious work
Muslim *(adj, n)* belonging to, or a person who believes in, the Islamic religion
Nawab, the an Indian prince
picnic a meal which is eaten in the open air somewhere away from home
pilgrimage a journey to a religious place or shrine
poem a piece of writing which expresses feelings in beautiful words
pregnant having a baby growing inside the body
protect to look after, to defend
relaxed *(adj)* feeling comfortable and unworried
religion a belief in a god or gods
robe a long, loose dress or piece of clothing
Sahib a title that was used when speaking to an important man in India
scandal action or behaviour which people think is wrong or shameful
servant a person who is paid to do housework
shrine a religious or holy place
shutters metal or wooden covers for windows, to keep out the heat and light
spirit the soul, the part of a person that is not the body, and that some people believe does not die
statue a figure of a person made of stone, or metal, etc.

string a very thin kind of rope; we use string to tie parcels
temple a building used for religious ceremonies
threat *(n)* a warning that you will punish or harm somebody if they do not do what you want
threaten *(n)* to make a threat
treatment (medical) something done by doctors to cure an illness
Urdu an Indian language

ACTIVITIES

Before Reading

1 **Read 'About the Story' on the first page. What do you know now about the differences between the two women? Find the best words to complete these sentences.**

1 Olivia was _____ to a British official, who was working in _____. She was _____ with her rather dull life, and felt _____. In _____ her life changed dramatically, and there was a _____.

2 The narrator is a _____ young Englishwoman, who is independent, and _____ to do what she wants. She is _____ about Olivia's past, so _____ years later she also goes to Satipur.

2 **Most of the story takes place in India. Read 'The British in India' on the first page, and answer these questions.**

1 Who controlled India in 1923?
2 Who kept law and order in India at that time?
3 When did India become independent?
4 What happened to most British officials in India after that?

3 **Can you guess what might happen to the two women in the story? Circle Y (Yes) or N (No) for each of these possibilities.**

1 Both the women learn a lot from living in India. Y/N
2 The single woman has a sexual relationship with someone. Y/N
3 The married woman finds a job and becomes independent. Y/N
4 The woman from the past influences the life of the woman in the present. Y/N
5 Both the women die in India. Y/N

ACTIVITIES

While Reading

Read the Introduction on pages 1 to 3. Choose the best question-word for these questions, and then answer them.

What / When / Who / Whose

1 . . . story is it, according to the narrator?
2 . . . was Douglas Rivers' job?
3 . . . came as a shock to the British in Satipur in September 1923?
4 . . . were the parents of the narrator's father?
5 . . . is the narrator's relationship to Olivia?
6 . . . never visited Tessie and Beth while Douglas was alive?
7 . . . letters were given first to Harry, then Tessie and Beth, and finally the narrator?

Read to the end of the Diary on page 37, and answer these questions.

Narrator's Story

1 Which Indian city did the narrator first arrive in?
2 What useful advice did she receive from a missionary?
3 Who was Inder Lal?
4 Why was the Nawab's palace empty now?
5 Why had Chid come to India?
6 What could Mrs Saunders see from the back of her house?
7 How did Inder Lal's mother help the narrator?
8 What did Hindu women ask for, at Baba Firdaus' shrine?
9 Why did the narrator get angry with Chid?
10 Who went on a pilgrimage into the mountains, and why?

Olivia's Story

1 Why was Olivia so bored in Satipur?
2 What did she realize as soon as she met the Nawab?
3 Why did Douglas refuse the Nawab's invitation to dinner?
4 What did Olivia find out about the Nawab's wife?
5 Who built Baba Firdaus' shrine, and why?
6 Why did Harry want to return to England?

Before you read on, what do you think will happen to the relationships between these people?

- The narrator and Chid
- The narrator and Inder Lal
- Olivia and Douglas
- Olivia and the Nawab
- The Nawab and Douglas
- The Nawab and Harry

Read to the end of Olivia's Story on page 71. Who said this, and to whom? Who or what were they talking about?

Olivia's Story

1 'People are always ready to tell lies.'
2 'They can't manage without us.'
3 'You shouldn't keep coming. You shouldn't be here.'
4 'That can't be true. He wouldn't do that.'
5 'He's so stupid. I almost feel sorry for him.'
6 'I feel like a man in the desert who has just found water.'
7 'Then why did you make me tie the string? It wasn't necessary!'

Narrator's Story

1 'I'm not surprised you laugh at us.'
2 'He always needed money and he didn't care how he got it.'
3 'But then where should she die?'
4 'They can tell each other the secrets they keep in their hearts.'

Read to the end of the Diary at the top of page 82. Are these sentences true (T) or false (F)? Rewrite the false sentences with the correct information.

Narrator's Story

1 Maji advised the narrator not to have an abortion.
2 Inder Lal was delighted to hear about the narrator's pregnancy.
3 Chid finally lost interest in India.
4 The narrator decided she wanted to have a baby.

Olivia's Story

1 Olivia told her husband about her pregnancy first.
2 The Nawab was suspected of organizing gangs of robbers.
3 When the Nawab's father died, the English dancer who had lived with him was poisoned by the Begum.
4 Olivia knew exactly who her baby's father was.
5 Olivia decided to have an abortion.

Before you finish the story, what do you think happens in the end? Circle Y (Yes) or N (No) for each of these possibilities.

Olivia's Story

1 The Begum refuses to help Olivia get an abortion. Y/N
2 Olivia tries to make Douglas take her back. Y/N
3 Olivia stays in India but doesn't live with the Nawab. Y/N
4 The Nawab dies in the Begum's arms. Y/N
5 The Nawab marries Olivia and they have other children. Y/N

Narrator's Story

1 The narrator lives in the mountains, near Olivia's house. Y/N
2 The narrator finds out a lot about the rest of Olivia's life. Y/N
3 The narrator returns to England to have her baby. Y/N

ACTIVITIES

After Reading

1 **Who's who? Match the characters to their names, and then to the sentences below.**

Tessie	Mr Crawford's assistant
Inder Lal	wife of the narrator's landlord
The Nawab	the Nawab's British friend
Ritu	the narrator's landlord
Maji	Douglas's first wife
Sandy Cabobpur	the Prince of Khatm
The Begum	a British traveller
Douglas	Douglas's second wife
Chid	an Indian holy woman
Olivia	the Nawab's wife
Harry	the Nawab's mother

1 . . . wanted more excitement in her life.
2 . . . could make surprising things happen, possibly by magic.
3 . . . believed that all possessions should be shared.
4 . . . had very good self-control and never showed his feelings.
5 . . . was worried about an ageing relation.
6 . . . was not mentally strong enough to stay with her husband.
7 . . . made most of the final decisions at the Palace.
8 . . . had more in common with her husband than his first wife had.
9 . . . did not seem to enjoy having a family.
10 . . . did not like being given advice by the British.
11 . . . was too shy to have a conversation with a stranger.

2 Here are parts of four letters written by people in the story. Choose one suitable word to fill each gap, and say who wrote each letter. Which order were the letters written in, and what had just happened before each letter was written?

Olivia (to her sister Marcia) / The Begum (to Harry's mother)
The narrator (to Tessie Rivers) / Harry (to the Nawab)

1 . . . They are such close friends that _____ dear son wishes to stay a _____ longer with us, but, as a _____ myself, I know how sad you _____ feel that he is not coming _____. So I have great pleasure in _____ you to join us at the _____, to stay as long as you _____. And remember that you now have _____ one son but two, and that _____ your sons are eager for your _____.

2 Today I went with a friend _____ see the palace, which has been _____ for years. It was hard to _____ it as Olivia had known it, _____ the Nawab gave parties for the _____. There was nothing left in those _____ white rooms except two old broken _____ and a silk curtain. It was _____ sad, really . . .

3 Mr and Mrs Rivers have very _____ invited me to stay until the _____ in Khatm is over, so I _____ sending this note back with your _____. Please _____ be upset – I know you think _____ is no danger, but I feel _____ safer here . . .

4 . . . You see, I feel I am _____ to know the *real* India now, _____ I am spending more time with _____, like the Nawab. And yesterday was _____ fun! He told me about the _____, and then we had a lovely _____ in the shade of some tall _____, with a cool stream at our _____. Such a relief after the terrible _____ of the car!

3 **After Mr Crawford and Douglas had both died, Beth Crawford felt able to answer the narrator's questions about Olivia (see pages 1 and 3). Complete the narrator's part of the conversation.**

NARRATOR: __________

BETH: Oh, she was a pretty young thing, of course, but not very intelligent, I'm afraid.

NARRATOR: __________

BETH: Well, she believed everything the Nawab told her, for a start! She wouldn't listen to a word any of us said against him!

NARRATOR: __________

BETH: In love! Well, perhaps she thought she was. But *he* wasn't in love with *her* – oh no, he was just using her, we all knew that.

NARRATOR: __________

BETH: Because he wanted to get his revenge on the British, of course! And what better way than to cause a scandal like that?

NARRATOR: __________

BETH: Oh, Dr Saunders told his wife, she told someone else, and soon we all knew. It was such a shock! And imagine – for weeks Olivia let poor Douglas think it was *his* child!

NARRATOR: __________

BETH: Nonsense, dear. Why else did she have an abortion? Harry said that awful old woman, the Begum, arranged it all.

NARRATOR: __________

BETH: Who knows? Perhaps she thought poor Douglas would shoot her darling son when he found out whose baby it was.

NARRATOR: __________

BETH: He never said a word about it, just got on with his job.

NARRATOR: __________

BETH: No, never. None of us ever saw her again, thank goodness.

4 Do you agree (A) or disagree (D) with these ideas? Explain why.

1 Douglas could have prevented Olivia from falling in love with the Nawab, by paying her more attention.
2 Harry should have returned home to his mother earlier.
3 Olivia was right to have the abortion.
4 The reason Olivia went to the Nawab's palace after leaving hospital was simply that she had nowhere else to go.
5 The Nawab had to buy Olivia a house outside Khatm, because the Begum would not have wanted Olivia to live in the palace.
6 The Nawab lost interest in Olivia after she had left Douglas.
7 Olivia's lonely life in the mountains was a kind of punishment for breaking the rules of society.
8 The narrator should have told Inder Lal she was pregnant.
9 The narrator should have gone back to England when she realized she was pregnant, to be looked after by her family.
10 It was a mistake for an Englishman like Chid to try to become an Indian holy man.

5 As a title, *Heat and Dust* gives us a picture of India. What titles would suggest the times, cultures, or relationships in this story? Use the words below to invent some new titles. Which title do you like best for this story? Why?

fifty years / the past / love / change / echo / view / mountain / Indian / India / British / England / prince / palace / the Sahib / the Nawab / shrine / picnic / pilgrimage

Now think of a title for a story set in your country (or another one), which uses two words joined by 'and', like *Heat and Dust*.

6 In what ways are the narrator and Olivia similar or different? Make sentences about them, using these phrases to help you.

- ordinary Indian people of the town / closed society of British officials in India
- a simple, economical lifestyle / elegant clothes and furniture
- sexual relationship with an Indian / neighbours don't mind / cause a scandal
- get close to the 'real' India / choose to stay there / perhaps no choice / happy or unhappy
- having an Indian baby / no problem in the 1970s / very shocking for British circle
- independent / own decisions / own money / dependent / man / living expenses

7 What did Olivia think about, up there in the mountains, for the last thirty-six years of her life? Here are four diary entries she might have written in 1954, a year after the Nawab's death. Complete each entry in the most suitable way.

1 How quiet and peaceful my life is now! I shall never see England again, but I don't think I would want to. I have everything I could wish for here . . .

2 Why did he die? Why did he leave me like that? I gave up everything for him! I'll never get away from here now . . .

3 It was all worth it, all the shame and scandal. But I still wish I'd had the baby. He'd be twenty-one by now. I wonder what he would have looked like? Perhaps he . . .

4 How sad and lonely my life is! I have no friends, nothing to do all day, nothing to look at but these cold mountains. I wish . . .

Which diary entry do *you* think Olivia would have written?

ABOUT THE AUTHOR

Ruth Prawer Jhabvala was born in 1927 in Germany, of Polish parents. Her first stories were written in German, but when her family moved to England in 1939, she rapidly made the change to a new language. After graduating from the University of London, she married an Indian architect and moved to Delhi, where she had three daughters, and wrote eight novels based on her experience of life in India. The first ten years of India, she has said, were wonderful, but then she became homesick for Europe and began to write more like an outsider, looking at the country and its people from a distance. Since 1975 she has divided her time between New York, Delhi, and London.

She has written twelve novels and several collections of short stories, which have been highly praised. In 1963 she wrote her first screenplay, based on her own novel *The Householder*, for a film directed by James Ivory. Since then she has been a regular member of the Merchant–Ivory team, writing screenplays for many successful films, like *Shakespeare Wallah, Quartet, A Room with a View, Howards End, The Remains of the Day*, and *Surviving Picasso*. Her best-known novel, *Heat and Dust*, was published in 1975, winning her the valuable Booker prize, and she wrote the screenplay for the film, which came out in 1983. (Stills from the film illustrate this book.)

Jhabvala has described her work as 'a two-way traffic' in which 'what I have learned in films I put back into my books, and what I have learned about . . . writing fiction I've put to use in writing films. I can't think what it would have been like for me to have had one and not the other.'

ABOUT BOOKWORMS

OXFORD BOOKWORMS LIBRARY

Classics • True Stories • Fantasy & Horror • Human Interest
Crime & Mystery • Thriller & Adventure

The OXFORD BOOKWORMS LIBRARY offers a wide range of original and adapted stories, both classic and modern, which take learners from elementary to advanced level through six carefully graded language stages:

Stage 1 (400 headwords)	**Stage 4** (1400 headwords)
Stage 2 (700 headwords)	**Stage 5** (1800 headwords)
Stage 3 (1000 headwords)	**Stage 6** (2500 headwords)

More than fifty titles are also available on cassette, and there are many titles at Stages 1 to 4 which are specially recommended for younger learners. In addition to the introductions and activities in each Bookworm, resource material includes photocopiable test worksheets and Teacher's Handbooks, which contain advice on running a class library and using cassettes, and the answers for the activities in the books.

Several other series are linked to the OXFORD BOOKWORMS LIBRARY. They range from highly illustrated readers for young learners, to playscripts, non-fiction readers, and unsimplified texts for advanced learners.

Oxford Bookworms Starters
Oxford Bookworms Playscripts
Oxford Bookworms Factfiles
Oxford Bookworms Collection

Details of these series and a full list of all titles in the OXFORD BOOKWORMS LIBRARY can be found in the *Oxford English* catalogues. A selection of titles from the OXFORD BOOKWORMS LIBRARY can be found on the next pages.

BOOKWORMS • HUMAN INTEREST • STAGE 5

The Bride Price

BUCHI EMECHETA

Retold by Rosemary Border

When her father dies, Aku-nna and her young brother have no one to look after them. They are welcomed by their uncle because of Aku-nna's 'bride price' – the money that her future husband will pay for her.

In her new, strange home one man is kind to her and teaches her to become a woman. Soon they are in love, although everyone says he is not a suitable husband for her. The more the world tries to separate them, the more they are drawn together – until, finally, something has to break.

BOOKWORMS • HUMAN INTEREST • STAGE 5

Jeeves and Friends

P. G. WODEHOUSE

Retold by Clare West

What on earth would Bertie Wooster do without Jeeves, his valet? Jeeves is calm, tactful, resourceful, and has the answer to every problem. Bertie, a pleasant young man but a bit short of brains, turns to Jeeves every time he gets into trouble. And Bertie is *always* in trouble.

These six stories include the most famous of P. G. Wodehouse's memorable characters. There are three stories about Bertie and Jeeves, and three about Lord Emsworth, who, like Bertie, is often in trouble, battling with his fierce sister Lady Constance, and his even fiercer Scottish gardener, the red-bearded Angus McAllister . . .

BOOKWORMS • HUMAN INTEREST • STAGE 5

The Garden Party and Other Stories

KATHERINE MANSFIELD

Retold by Rosalie Kerr

Oh, how delightful it is to fall in love for the first time! How exciting to go to your first dance when you are a girl of eighteen! But life can also be hard and cruel, if you are young and inexperienced and travelling alone across Europe . . . or if you are a child from the wrong social class . . . or a singer without work and the rent to be paid.

Set in Europe and New Zealand, these nine stories by Katherine Mansfield dig deep beneath the appearances of life to show us the causes of human happiness and despair.

BOOKWORMS • CLASSICS • STAGE 5

Far from the Madding Crowd

THOMAS HARDY

Retold by Clare West

Bathsheba Everdene is young, proud, and beautiful. She is an independent woman and can marry any man she chooses – if she chooses. In fact, she likes her independence, and she likes fighting her own battles in a man's world.

But it is never wise to ignore the power of love. There are three men who would very much like to marry Bathsheba. When she falls in love with one of them, she soon wishes she had kept her independence. She learns that love brings misery, pain, and violent passions that can destroy lives . . .

BOOKWORMS • THRILLER & ADVENTURE • STAGE 5

This Rough Magic

MARY STEWART

Retold by Diane Mowat

The Greek island of Corfu lies like a jewel, green and gold, in the Ionian sea, where dolphins swim in the sparkling blue water. What better place for an out-of-work actress to relax for a few weeks?

But the island is full of danger and mysteries, and Lucy Waring's holiday is far from peaceful. She meets a rude young man, who seems to have something to hide. Then there is a death by drowning, and then another . . .

BOOKWORMS • HUMAN INTEREST • STAGE 6

Dublin People

MAEVE BINCHY

Retold by Jennifer Bassett

A young country girl comes to live and work in Dublin. Jo is determined to be modern and independent, and to have a wonderful time. But life in a big city is full of strange surprises for a shy country girl . . .

Gerry Moore is a man with a problem – alcohol. He knows he must give it up, and his family and friends watch nervously as he battles against it. But drink is a hard enemy to fight . . .

These stories by the Irish writer Maeve Binchy are full of affectionate humour and wit, and sometimes a little sadness.